Sweet Victory

by

Angela Kay Austin

Vanilla Heart Publishing
USA

Sweet Victory
by Angela Kay Austin

Copyright 2011 Angela Kay Austin

Published by: Vanilla Heart Publishing
www.VanillaHeartBookAndAuthors.com
10121 Evergreen Way, 25-156
Everett, WA 98204 USA

ISBN-13: 978-0615905457   ISBN-10: 0615905455

10 9 8 7 6 5 4 3 2 Second Edition

First Printing, October 2013
Printed in the United States of America

Sweet Victory

by

Angela Kay Austin

Dedication

Today's economy has changed many people's lives, myself included. When there is forced change in your life...how do you handle it?

Recently, my brother was laid-off. Awe-struck, I watched his determination and struggle to provide for his family and take care of himself. Whenever I asked him how he kept it going he simply said "...another day, Sis, another day."

I dedicate this book to my brother and to anyone who has been affected by today's economy. All it ever takes is another day.

Acknowledgements

In January, I was laid-off; it changed my life. Of course, financially, but also as one of my closest friends says "...the trajectory..." of my life. I thought I knew where I was going.

When you are 18 a fresh start is exciting. At 21, a new beginning feels like the world is opening up to you. At 35, 40, or 50 it's not necessarily as thrilling. It might even be a little scary.

For this book, I wanted to investigate "starting over" at 30. And what if the options available to you are not the options you want?

People tire of listening to you whine, uhh I mean research your feelings. But, I'm grateful that my girlfriends and family never did.

Chris and Keni have not only been inspirational, they have been dependable sounding boards for all of my frustrations as I peeled back the layers of myself to tell the story of Victoria James.

Thank you to everyone that sent me leads on jobs, articles about the economy, etc. All of it meant the world to me.

Chapter One

The mountains looming on the horizon shadowed the highway speckled beige by the light of overhead lampposts. They had been Victoria Marie James' main companions for the past thirteen hours. The navigational system mounted in her dashboard sang at her with every turn. The relentless voice pointed out her inability to find the right exit an hour outside of Memphis—her childhood hometown. One five-minute break at a rest stop for a quick cup of coffee—now, staining her gray jogging pants—was turning into a nightmare. *Automatic updates my ass.* The red and blue lights in her rearview mirror followed by short bursts of a siren were God sent. She pulled onto the shoulder of 240 West and waited.

The officer dismounted his motorcycle, and approached her. It was after 2:00 A.M., and she'd exhausted herself turning in circles for the last thirty minutes. She didn't know what she was doing. Memphis, Tennessee was only so big. The familiar gait of the backlit figure approaching her car knotted her stomach. *Chad Michael Kirkpatrick.* There was no way fate could be so cruel.

When her window slid down, she stared at the beautiful blond curls peeking from underneath the helmet, highlighting brown eyes. She remembered a time when he preferred glasses, but thought they might be uncomfortable under his helmet.

"License and registration, please."

With a steely glare, he waited as she rooted around in her glove box, and then her wallet. She glanced at his nametag—Kirkpatrick, and back into his eyes several times as she handed him both items. What was she supposed to say or do? Eventually, she knew she'd have to face him, but not after nearly fourteen hours in a car surrounded by trash from Slim Jims, fast food, and coffee cups. And really not while wearing stained clothing. Their fingers brushed in the exchange. Goodness, such a simple touch, but it flooded her with so many memories. Not all of them good. *God, how could she have hurt him so badly?*

With an exhale, her back straightened, thrusting forward her small bosom; she quickly lifted then dropped her shoulders, but said nothing. Simply rested her hands in her lap, and sat quietly. *Was she shaking off his touch, his memory, or did she simply not care at all?* "Vic-Ms. James, I noticed you circling. Are you lost?"

"Yes, I am, Officer Kirkpatrick."

Officer Kirkpatrick. Usually, the formality is expected, but this time it wasn't nor was it wanted. He watched her fingers fiddle with the gauges on her dash, running across them as she spoke.

She glanced at the GPS embedded in her dashboard, and thumped it. "For some reason, this dumb thing is not putting me where I need to be."

He knew exactly where she was headed, but if she

wasn't going to say anything then neither was he. "So, where are you going? Maybe, I can help you find it." He handed her back her papers.

"I just need to find Elvis Presley Boulevard so I can get over to Lamar, but the freaking GPS keeps dumping me back onto the highway. Now, I need gas."

She wasn't talking about anything they couldn't fix, but he watched as her eyes began to glisten with tears. Where was she coming from, anyway? And where was her husband or boyfriend—fiancé? That's what the high school newsletter had called him: fiancé.

He nodded at the road ahead. "Ms. James, if you get off at the exit ahead of you there's a gas station. Once you gas up and get back on the highway continue south. About ten miles down you'll see the exit you need." He handed her a card. "If you get lost again, call me."

She took the card; read it, and again looked into his eyes. The connection lasted only moments before she turned away. He pulled down his visor, and turned to mount his bike and leave. He watched as she pulled her car back onto the road before he turned back to his hideaway tucked between trees and construction. Victoria was back, and from the size of the trailer hitched to the back of her car, it looked like she planned to stay. Why? As he flicked off his lights, he decided it didn't matter. She had acted as if they were strangers, and driven off without a hi or bye.

In twelve years he hadn't forgotten her. How could he stop thinking about her, now that he'd seen her again? Ensconced in his shrouded hideaway, he remembered it all. High school. Their child. *Almost.* Why torture himself about something *she* stopped before it could even begin? He tried to push it all out of his mind, but from the soulful gospel music playing in the background to the trash littered through the car to her aloofness, she wasn't the same.

He checked his watch. Soon his overtime would be

finished, and he could go home and crash.   Every day, for the past two weeks, he'd pulled some kind of overtime or worked at one of his part-time jobs.   He needed every penny.

Wind buzzed around Chad's helmet as he pushed his bike to its limits.   He knew he shouldn't, but he was tired, and he wanted to be at home in his favorite chair in front of the TV.   Grab a sandwich and sleep for about ten hours. The call dispatch sent across the radio meant he had to double back before he made his way to the station.   Damn. He really could use some sleep.   The overtime and Paige's tuition were killing him.

The dispatcher's call sent him to a neighborhood which had a record number of calls every night: domestic violence, car thefts, break-ins, and a few robberies.

A gas station attendant approached him before he could get off his bike.   The woman's thinning hair, frail frame, and caked on make-up probably aged her by fifteen years.   Overhead fluorescent lights glared across her ashen leathery skin highlighting a rainbow of stains soiling her uniform.   The spunk in her step and slight flirtatious smile confirmed she was younger than she looked.   Her name tag spelled Jenny.

"Officer."   The gap in her front teeth caused her Cs to have a hissing sound.   "Officer, the gal inside needs your help. She done gone and got her car stolen."

He scanned the area, but saw nothing.   No broken glass, sticks, rocks, nothing. "Ma'am, where is she?"

"Inside. I gave 'er some water to calm 'er nerves."

In this part of town, no one ever had working cameras,

but he asked anyway. "Are your cameras working?"

"No, sir, but I saw a lot."

"Okay, let me talk to the victim first, and then I'll want to talk to you, too."

Jenny walked through the doors ahead of him. When she stepped to the side, he saw her. Victoria. What the hell was she doing here? He'd sent her to a gas station in a completely different direction. It'd been twelve years since she'd lived in Memphis, but did she really not remember anything. Or did she want to forget everything?

Puffy red eyes stared blankly at rows of chips. Her body went limp like a deflated balloon; she slid from the folding chair onto the floor. He ran—too slow—and watched her head hit the floor.

Crouching at her side, he removed his helmet and gloves and smoothed away the black curls covering her eyes. He propped her head up with the jacket he wore. Her eyes flickered open as his fingers checked her wrist for a pulse.

Slowly, she woke. "Mikey."

Mikey. No one had called him Mikey since she left town. "You okay?" He scanned her body. His fingers slid from her forehead down her cheek. "How's your head?" Creases in her forehead softened.

"I'm okay." She tried to push herself off the floor. "What happened?"

He jerked his hand from her wrist, and gently pressed it against her heart to stop her from rising. Her heartbeat quickened beneath his touch. "Stay here for a moment. You fainted and hit your head. Give it a minute." Silently she complied with his request. "Are you okay?" She closed her eyes, and nodded in silence. "Do you need me to call an ambulance?"

"No, I'm okay." She covered his hand with hers, and tried to push from the floor again. This time he helped her ease into a

Sweet Victory

sitting position.

"Is there someone you want me to call?"

"No. No one."

No one. "What about Gramps?" *Your fiancé?*

Her grip on his hand tightened. "Please no. I don't want him to worry."

"Okay. Can you tell me what happened?"

She looked at him; her pinched expression replaced—with what? Relief? Happiness? He wasn't sure, but it made him want to never let her leave his side again. "Mikey." She threw her arms around his neck. "They took everything." Soft sobs hiccupped against his neck.

Jenny stared at them wide-eyed before she turned and walked back behind the counter to busy herself cleaning the coffee maker.

"Mikey, my car. My stuff. They got everything."

Through his layers of Kevlar he felt the old familiar warmth of her. Hair scented of aloe flooded his senses. This time she wasn't a dream that faded with the buzz of his alarm clock, but the car and things she cried about were not *his* Victory. The belt he wore loaded with everything from his radio to his gun stopped him from getting as close as he would have liked. "Victoria, slow down. Tell me what happened."

She loosened her grip on his neck, and he helped her from the floor back into the chair. He knelt in front of her. "Mikey, I'm sorry about earlier."

"It's okay. Victoria, tell me what happened."

"Why didn't you say something?"

"I didn't think you wanted me to."

She cocked her head to the side like she used to, and

said nothing for a moment. In a flash, he remembered every moment he'd seen that before: during tests, when they were studying, or playing board games. Anytime she needed to figure something out. "That was a long time ago."

"Yeah, twelve years. So, tell me what happened."

She looked around the store, retracing her steps. "After I paid for my gas, I went to the bathroom. Down the candy aisle, past the drinks..."—she looked at him for a moment—"...while I was in there, I realized I'd left my key on the counter when I took the bathroom key from the cashier. By the time I ran out someone else had walked in, picked up my keys, and left." Her head fell into her hands. "God, I don't know where my head is." Her shoulders bounced with silent sobs, and then a petite balled fist slammed into the side of the chair. "What am I gonna do now?"

He grabbed her hand and held it. "Don't worry, we'll fix this." The pads of his fingers ran across the purplish bruise forming on the side of her fist. "Everything will be okay." *Damn.* He almost brought her hand to his lips and kissed it. *What the hell was he thinking?* Her hand fell to her lap from his as if on fire.

Victoria's tear-filled eyes focused on him. Her loss and pain were beginning to make him act stupid. It took too many years for him to put her and their past behind him. He stood to move away, but he couldn't stop staring into her watery hazel eyes.

How many times had he heard of someone doing something stupid like leaving a key under a mat or hiding jewelry in an underwear drawer or giving a friend their ATM PIN? People always ended up getting taken in those instances, but walking away from your key in a store. The word "intelligent" barely began to describe Victoria back when he knew her. Honor Society. Drama Club. Cheerleader. What was going on with her that she'd walk away from her car keys? "Victoria, you wait here. Let me talk to Jenny.   Do you want anything more to drink?"

"No."   Victoria sat with a vacant expression in her eyes. Slumped in the chair, defeated, she seemed to be thinking or looking at nothing.   Just sipping from the bottle of water.

He approached Jenny at the counter.   "Can you give me an accurate description of the person or people involved?"

"I only had one customer after her, and he was one of the neighborhood kids.   I think his name is Jamal.   Jamal somethin'. 'bout foteen or so."

"Do you know where he lives?"

"Nawh, but he be in here all the time."

Jenny didn't have all the details, but she knew enough. It wouldn't take him long to find Jamal.   He hoped he could find him before somebody stripped down Victoria's car and sold every part, maxed out every credit card, and fenced every possession in her moving truck.   He broadcast a lookout for her car and truck, and wondered where she would sleep tonight.

After breaking the sound barrier returning to the district, Chad had gone back to the gas station where he'd left Victoria.   As promised, Jenny had watched over her. Providing her with orange juice and conversation.   As soon as he returned, she gathered up Victoria's leftovers, and helped them to the car.

His tiny one bedroom, Paige's domain when she visited, wasn't big enough for them, let alone him and Victoria, but where else was he going to take Victoria?   He couldn't afford to put her in a hotel, and her purse was gone, locked in the trunk for safety. How would she pay for it herself? So, he stripped the dirty sheets from his bed, shoved dolls, games, and books into a toy chest, and cleaned up the bathroom. He left Victoria in the tiny overstuffed room, and made up the couch for himself.

When he went back to the bedroom to check on her, she was sitting at the foot of the bed, head hung with her hands tucked between her knees. Quiet and sad.

His words were soft. In his mind, he pictured her crumbling at the sound of his voice. "Victoria, I know you're tired, but we need to contact your banks and credit card companies. I think we'll find your car and hopefully your stuff fast, but they might try to use your cards over the Internet or at stores where they have friends."

Dazed, her expression latched onto him. He'd only seen the hurt in her eyes once before, and he'd promised himself then he'd never see it again, but here it was. Big beautiful hazel eyes stared at him. Tangled shoulder length curls surrounded her pear-shaped face. He glanced around the room for a piece of paper and a pen. Paige's colored pencils and drawing paper were the best he could find. The bed squeaked and shifted under his weight. "Victoria, write down the names of your banks and credit card companies for me."

She took the red pencil, and began to write. Her hand was steady, but she still didn't speak. The list she jotted down was thankfully short: two credit cards, and two bank cards. The bank cards he called first, and then the credit card companies. The second card he left open because there had been activity. Eventually, the activity would lead him to Jamal. The customer service department was more than happy to work with an officer in tracking down the stolen card. The calls were easy enough to make, and at least he wouldn't have to worry about all her money vanishing.

Sweet Victory

"Victoria, you need to sleep." Again, he examined the dark circles under her eyes, and her droopy shoulders. The healthy glow of her sandy brown skin was gone. "I need to take care of a few things." He placed a hand on each of her shoulders, and twisted her toward him. "Will you be okay? Do you need anything?"

"Don't leave me, Mikey." His name coming out of her mouth warmed parts of him it shouldn't. He fought the urges inside of him to wipe away the tears from her lips with his own.

The pain and exhaustion in her voice cut right through him. "I'll be back. I just want to check on some things."

Her arms circled his waist, and she rested her head on his chest. "Lie beside me. I don't want to be alone."

For twelve years, he'd wanted another opportunity to lie beside her, but now he couldn't take advantage of it because if he did, he might be unable to catch Jamal before he sold everything she owned. And because this time he would not be able to let her walk away. He reached around to where her hands locked together behind his back, and gently, but firmly pulled them apart. Soft curls brushed against his chin. A hint of aloe overtook him. Memories of burying his fingers into those curls, and her scent on his body flooded through him. He needed to get out, get away, before he made a fool of himself, again. "I'll be back."

He rummaged through his closet, and found a t-shirt. He inspected it; once navy blue, now it was more of a dingy blue, maybe gray. The orange logo on the left breast chipped more with each wash, but it was still one of his favorite shirts. As he handed it to her, he hoped it was long enough to cover any part of her tempting body. Then he glanced at legs nearly as long as his own. No way.

"Mikey." The single word hung on her tongue.

Her spending the night was a bad idea. Why did she

say his name like *that*?   He hesitated in the doorway. "Victory..."—a name he hadn't used in a long time.   A name he and her grandparents would yell at competitions and games to support her.   "Victory, don't worry.   I'll take care of everything.   I'll be back, soon."

Chapter Two

Tracking down the kid who had walked away with everything important to Victoria had taken Chad and his partner all night. First, Wal-Mart, then, an all-night grocery, and now, he'd stopped for food at a local carry-out. Oddly enough, the grocery had been Chad's best lead. Their camera worked, and the cashier knew Jamal Echols.

Chad's partner, Alex Myles, pulled up to the carry-out and parked. It was in the same neighborhood as the gas station. Jenny had been close, but Jamal was actually sixteen, and he'd already been in and out of juvie. Like too many others who had made his job hard, not because of what they did, but because of who they were—children—Jamal's parents were missing in action. Both had their own histories in and out of jail. Without their guidance and he guessed nothing or no one else positive to replace them, Jamal linked in with Memphis' growing gangs. The wrong kind of family, but a family.

Technically, Chad was off-duty, but Myles wasn't. He couldn't count the number of times Alex Myles had done him a favor that saved his ass. And he returned the favor just as often. Myles had been on the Memphis Police Department for almost twenty years. Five years ago, he'd trained Chad. Chad trusted him with his life. He stared at the chocolate complexioned man. Over the past years, he'd witnessed the man morph from a pre-retirement ball buster cop to a man on cruise control while he contemplated early retirement instead of working his last five years. Retiring to a warm climate with his wife was all the man talked about.

Myles and Chad strolled toward the diner. Each scanned the lot: looked for cars with passengers, unnecessary people hanging out, or any activity that would let them know whether Jamal was backed up by his gang or alone. Victoria's car was parked right up front by the glass. He guessed Jamal wanted to keep an eye on it before he scrapped it. Didn't want to give somebody else the chance to walk away with his prize.

The door chime tolled at their entry. After a nod from Myles, Chad casually walked to the register to speak with the cashier. They wanted to be sure no one else was going to surprise them from a backroom or bathroom. Myles continued to Jamal's table. The woman he sat with placed her hand on top of his, and said something Chad couldn't hear. The kid nodded, and kept stuffing chicken in his face.

Myles flashed his badge. "Jamal Echols. You're a person of interest in an investigation. I need you to come with me."

The young woman with her back to Myles spoke. "He has to come with you for what?" She turned to face Myles. "What did he do?"

"Ma'am, who are you?" Myles wasn't about to waste his time.

Chad wanted the kid, so he could finally go home. Twenty-four hours without sleep was nipping at his eyelids. From where he stood, he couldn't make out her expression. But, she hesitated before she spoke, wiping her mouth with her fingers. "I'm a family friend."

"A family friend?"

Chad walked over, and stood beside the woman; Myles

rounded the table to Jamal. Myles and Chad exchanged glances. The woman's words didn't ring true. Chad knew she wasn't his mother, but their dark skin, round eyes, and full lips definitely mirrored.

"Yes." Intricately designed fake nails scratched at tufts of black hair near her forehead. With each score her auburn wig moved back and forth.

Chad and Myles traded another 'yeah-right' glance. Technically, he was off duty, so he watched the interchange. "Well, family friend, unless you're a guardian, and can show proof, Jamal will be leaving with us, and you can let his family know," said Myles.

Myles dropped his card on the table, grabbed Jamal by an arm, and lifted the boy from his seat. Mild mannered by nature, Myles' rounded physique usually hid his strength, and he liked it that way. Myles mirandized Jamal as he twisted the kid's arms behind his back. Jamal's eyes widened as the cuffs ratcheted into place. He stared at the nameless woman as if telepathically willing her to do something. For the first time since they'd found Jamal, he showed fear. At sixteen, if he went to jail this time, things might be different. It might not be juvie.

She used the card to pick chicken remnants from underneath her fingernails. Her eyebrows bunched together. Maybe from pain. Maybe from concern. "Where can we pick him up?" Then her tongue flicked in and out of her mouth. She made a loud sucking noise as she tried to dislodge food stuck between her teeth.

Myles nodded at the card in her hand. "You call the number on the card, and they'll let a lawyer or someone from the family know everything." Myles began to lead Jamal toward the door. Chad motioned at the car through the window. "Oh yeah, we'll need the keys to the car outside."

Flicking one of her shiny Pocahontas plaits over her shoulder, she glanced down at keys sprawled on the table.

Sweet Victory

The kid winced as Myles shifted him around; Myles grabbed the keys, and they exited. They sat in the lot until the tow truck showed up to get the car, and take it to the impound lot. Searching Jamal, they'd found Victoria's credit cards, and her purse was in the car, but the moving truck was gone. Chad was positive the woman at the table knew where it was, but so did Jamal. Maybe they'd get lucky and find something, but Jamal was a minor, and it would be hard with youth services slowing down everything. Good thing, Jamal's parents didn't care, so they had time.

Early the next morning, Chad woke to the smells of breakfast: bacon, eggs, syrup—molasses. He leaned over the side of the couch, and grabbed his cell phone. 11:30 in the morning. Only three hours of sleep. He threw his legs over the side of the couch, and followed his nose into the kitchen to find Victoria on her tiptoes trying to reach the plates on the top shelf.

His eyes scanned her long lean legs accented with muscular calves. The t-shirt he'd given her to sleep in rose up to her hips. It barely covered her bottom, and the boy cut panties she wore didn't hide anything either. "Mmm." Her back arched slightly, and her breasts thrust forward. She wasn't wearing a bra, but her small perky breasts didn't seem to need the support. His mouth began to water at the lure of much more than a hot breakfast. *Really, really crazy ass idea.*

Small ringlets flopped around her head when she turned, acknowledging his presence.

Wide-eyed, her mouth hung open for a moment before she spoke. "Good morning. After last night, I didn't think you'd be awake so soon."

He ran his hand through his hair. "I could say the same thing for you, but even *I* can't believe I'm awake." Eyeing the plates, he said, "Let me get those for you."

"Yeah, I didn't hear you come in, but I thought you might like some breakfast. I didn't mean to wake you. I'm sorry." She lowered herself to her bare feet, and stepped to the side allowing him as much room as she could in the small kitchen.

"Don't worry about it. I wanted to talk to you anyway." He knew she was anxious to know details, and he wanted to tell her. "But, I didn't want to wake you."

Victoria took the plates he handed her and loaded them with bacon, scrambled eggs, stretched with milk and cheese, and French toast. She really loved French toast, especially her grandmother's. Extra thick slices of homemade bread loaded with powdered sugar and cinnamon on top would be better. He had a few end pieces of wheat and potato bread, but it would do for today. For too long, she focused on the sugar topping, no cinnamon. But, what else was she going to do? Gawk at the half naked gorgeous guy staring at her like he wanted to put her on a plate? No, she couldn't stare because she might let him.

As she poured generous amounts of syrup on the French toast, he spoke.

"We found the kid that stole your car."

The glass syrup bottle slapped the countertop, and she threw her body into his. His hard chest pressed against her breasts. Hesitantly, his arms circled her waist, and she tightened her grip. She didn't think he'd found anything since he hadn't awakened her.

If nothing else, she could trade-in or sell her car. Along with her savings she might be okay until she figured out something else. "Thank you. Thank you."

She planted small kisses on his lips over and over. After a minute, she realized what she was doing, and stopped. *Whoa!* What on earth was she thinking? When she stepped out of his reluctant release and gazed into his eyes, the air in the room seemed to be sucked away. The intensity in them increased her desire for him, but made her even more aware of where she was, and who she was with. The man whose *baby* she... The sadness that had crammed her mind and heart as she'd driven for fourteen hours began to fill her to overload. With a deep breath, she smoothed her hands down her torso, wrapped them around herself, and then rested her butt against the countertop. "How did you do it?"

"We tracked the activity on one of your cards, and combined that with information from lo-jack which led us to a carry-out. I...we didn't just want the car, we wanted Jamal, and he had the car with him. Before he was bailed out, he told us he'd sold or pawned most of your stuff. We visited the pawn shops...'fall off the back of the truck' type of establishments, but your clothes and the small stuff we have no real way of tracking. Street hustlers."

Victoria heard him, but she couldn't believe he'd accomplished so much so fast. She stared at the tiny plate of food, and wondered how she could pay him back for what he'd done.

"You won't be able to get the car and stuff for a while; it's evidence. But I'll speed things up as much as I can." He leaned back against the wall in the small kitchen, bare-chested. Loose-fitted pajama bottoms hung low on his hips. Deeply defined ab muscles disappeared beneath the drawstring.

Without him, without her stuff, what would she do? She would have had to start over from scratch, and with her grandfather waiting for her, she didn't know how to thank him. She kissed *her* Mikey. Warm and soft, his lips welcomed her. They parted slightly, and she leaned in further. Their tongues touched, and she jumped. What was she doing? *Again.* "Thank you so much. I don't know how I'll ever pay you back for all of this. You really didn't have to do it." She couldn't resist the touch of his skin, and slid her hand along his bare arm. Her fingers tumbled over each muscle. The lower her hand slid, the more his back pushed against the wall behind him. She grasped his hand, and led him back to the couch where he'd slept.

When she left him his tense expression mellowed. Carrying his plate of food and a glass of apple juice, she returned. It was the only juice in the refrigerator. If he'd had champagne and orange juice she would've served Mimosas in celebration. Moments later, she returned with her own plate, and sat beside him.

Taking a bite of the French toast he said, "Mmm, if I'd known you were such a good cook, I would've asked you to cook for me years ago."

"Well, I wasn't as good years ago, but I definitely could've made this for you. My grandfather loved my French toast. It's my grandma's recipe."

"Of course. How's Gramps doing?" He licked syrup from his lips.

She swallowed hard. "Okay. He said he understands that we have to move back into the house because I can't afford the home anymore."

Warm and steady, his hand covered hers. "I'm sure he understands it's not your fault."

She didn't want him to take his hand away, but he did.

Sweet Victory

"I know, but I think they took good care of him, and I don't know if I can." She stuffed eggs in her mouth to shut herself up.

After finishing his plate, he leaned back into the cushions. His flat stomach gave no clue he'd eaten three pieces of French toast, and a plateful of eggs and bacon. Victoria stared at her own half eaten food. Her appetite was really horrible, lately. She snuggled into the cushions, and closed her eyes. The movements of the cushions as Chad pushed up to leave made her open her eyes.

"I'll put the plates away." He reached for her plate, too.

"Don't." She tapped his hand with hers, and pushed the plate back to the table. Tightening her grip on his arm, she pulled him back to the couch, wrapped her arms around his waist, and leaned into him. She needed him near. "Mikey just sit with me."

"Victoria-"

She shut him up with a snuggle. Her legs curled underneath her, and she tightened her hold on his waist. He tensed, but slowly relaxed. She didn't want to make him uncomfortable, but she missed him. Briefly, she thought about letting go, but then his arm slid from the cushion behind her to her waist, and his hand rested on her hip.

"Mikey, let's just rest for a while. Do you have to work?"

"No, not today. I thought about working overtime, but I don't have to go."

"Well, then, that's that. I just haven't been able to sleep much. I'm so tired."

His free hand sifted through her curls as her head rested underneath his chin. "Then sleep. I'm here, and I'm not leaving."

She placed a tiny kiss on his chest. His scent washed over her. A mixture of the breakfast they'd had, soap, and something she couldn't place. Rubber or plastic. "Until I can get my stuff back, the only things I can do are get the house keys from the management company, maybe get a little furniture for Gramps and me, and figure out what's next."

"So, the keys for the house weren't with the rest of your stuff?"

"No. I was going to stay in a hotel nearby. And pick up the keys today."

"Oh, okay. I can help if you want me to."

"You've done so much. I don't want to wear out my welcome."

"I want to help. It's no problem."

"Hmm, thank you, Mikey."

Hours later, after Mikey had run Victoria around town to pick up keys, buy two bedroom suites of furniture, a few lamps, and some kitchen supplies, they stood in the house she'd grown up in. Each dip into her savings hurt, but more needed to be done. Some of the old wood siding on the exterior needed to be repaired, but inside, the small rooms were well tended. Recent paint still scented every room. A few of the kitchen appliances were older, but they worked. She'd need to test the oven, but she desperately wanted to keep it. It was her grandmother's pride and joy. The wood floors needed to be buffed, but they were in great shape. Her grandmother had picked a beautiful mahogany because it reminded her of The Peabody Hotel, one of the oldest

Sweet Victory

hotels in Memphis.

Frozen in time, the modest home brought back memories. "Remember when we'd stay up all night watching movies until Gramps would have to literally kick you out?"

He stopped checking windows to respond. "Yeah, but then I'd just sneak back through your bedroom window, and we'd finish watching." He checked another lock. "You think he knew?"

"Knowing Gramps, probably."

She headed toward the kitchen for a glass of water. "Do you want anything to drink?"

"No, I'm fine." He checked his watch. "But, I should be going. I'm going to pick up some overtime tomorrow morning."

His words twisted her stomach in knots. She didn't want him to leave, but she was being ridiculous using his kindness to hold him hostage. He had his own life, and from the dolls and coloring books in the room where she'd slept, there was a lot of his life she didn't know anything about.

"I'm sorry, Chad, I didn't mean to take advantage.

He crossed the room toward her. His hand cupped the side of her face. "I told you that you could stay with me if you don't feel safe. You don't have anything to sleep on but an air mattress. Until your stuff arrives, you can stay with me." His eyes searched hers. "But, I've got to be at work at 4:00 A.M., so I can't stay."

The house was old and drafty, but it was her home, and she needed to get comfortable in it, again. She wanted to bring her grandfather home as soon as possible, and the house was not going to get ready by itself. "You better go. You need to work, and I need to clean."

"I can come by and help you when I get off."

32

He didn't need to worry about her. "You need your sleep. I'll whip this place into shape."

She hugged him as hard as she could because she wasn't sure when she'd see him again. When she was alone, the emptiness of the house beat down on her. She'd left D.C. with nothing, but that car, her savings, and the stuff in that moving truck. It was meant to help her start over. She crumbled to the cold wood floor. What was she thinking? How was she going to do this alone? Tears welled in her eyes. She didn't stop them from falling. On the floor in the middle of her grandparents' house, she sat and cried. God, how was she going to make this work?

Chapter Three

An old blue bandana held down fuzzy auburn curls littered with soapy puffs. Dressed in dust covered jeans and a t-shirt, accented with yellow rubber gloves up to her elbows, Victoria stood in the doorway wide-eyed, and curious.

Chad had rushed through all the property release paperwork because he'd wanted to get to her. He knew his surprise would bring a smile to her face. "I hope you still like Tex Mex because I thought I'd bring you dinner."

"Mikey." Her beautiful bright smile beamed. "Of course, I still love Tex Mex."

"Well, I got this from El Pollo Rico. We used to go when we were kids. Remember?"

"How could I forget?" She began to remove her gloves, and turned to head back inside.

"Wait."

"Huh?"

"That's not the only reason I'm here." He stepped to the side, so she could see behind him.

The glow he hadn't seen since she returned to Memphis lit up her face. "Oh my God. Mikey!" Tears streamed down her face as she ran into his arms, chips snapped between them.

"Why are you crying?"

"Mikey, I didn't think you'd find it. I don't know what to

Sweet Victory

say..." Her arms tightened around his neck.

"Victory, I know you needed this stuff back, but what I don't know is what is going on. I'm happy...really happy you're back, but why did you leave D.C.?"

"I promise, I will explain everything, but not right now. Okay?"

He couldn't force her to tell him what he wanted to know. There were some things he needed to tell her, too. "Okay. So, do you want to eat first or haul your stuff inside?"

She ran past him to the car. Like a kid she circled the car laughing. "It's not damaged." She stared at the moving truck. "What's in there?"

He puffed out his chest, and dragged out his words. "Oh, just a few televisions, laptop, a ton of books, and a few paintings."

"What about pots and a breadmaker?"

"Did I forget to mention those?"

She squealed, and jumped up and down, and then ran into his arms, again. "I hate to waste money, especially right now, but forget about Tex Mex takeout. I'm cooking for you."

"Well, how about you cook, and I'll start moving things inside."

Splayed hands waited for the brown-bagged dinner he held. "Perfect. Give me those." Before disappearing into the house, she glanced back over her shoulder. "Hey do you like swordfish?" Then she waved the idea off. "No, no. I know exactly what to cook. Shrimp, corn, sausage, red potatoes. How about that?"

"Sounds perfect."

"Ohh, and my grandmother's tea cakes for dessert."

He knew having her stuff returned would make her happy, but as he watched her bounce into the house, he knew the spring in her glide represented pure *joy*. He'd seen it at too many competitions and events before.

Hours later, hunger pangs gnawed at him. Victoria had directed him with each piece of her found treasure. As he placed everything, he realized she'd transformed the small home. White walls had been repainted to shades of gold, greens, or browns. The bedroom furniture had arrived, but until he had delivered her stuff no televisions had been in place, although entertainment centers awaited their return. Half-filled bookshelves sat both in her bedroom, and the living room. He nestled missing pieces among the others. The fixtures in the bathroom had been replaced with more modern units. Sweaty and tired, he followed the smell of shrimp and corn into the kitchen. The kitchen hadn't been redone, but every item had been cleaned to perfection.

"Oh, man, that smells good." He stepped up behind her, one arm slid in place around her hip. She gazed up at him, and kissed him on the cheek.

"Thank you. Everything will be finished in a moment." She nodded at the bathroom. "Go and clean up, and I'll set the table."

Jazzy saxophone beats reverberated through the small home. The low ceilings enhanced the sound. Victoria slid an oblong tray loaded with golden corn on the cob, skewered shrimp, roasted red potatoes, and smoked turkey sausage in front of Mikey with the goal of making his mouth water.

She sat across the table watching him.

"What's up?" he asked.

Sweet Victory

"Nothing. Just watching you eat."

Juice dribbled down his chin as he bit into an ear of corn.

Her plate sat untouched. "Do you like it?"

She waited patiently for his response.

"Yes." He popped a shrimp into his mouth. "This is delicious."

With a sigh, she nibbled on a piece of sausage. "I'm glad."

After hours of laughter and food, they sat at the table over crumb-filled plates. Vanilla and sugar lingered in the air and her mouth from the tea cakes.

"I can't remember when I've eaten that good. Thanks." He checked his watch. "It's getting late. I should be heading home."

She rose and cleared away the dishes. "We could watch a movie," she said from the kitchen. "Until Gramps is moved back in, I have a spare room."

"You want me to stay the night?"

"I just mean if you're sleepy after the movie, you could crash."

She heard him as he twisted around in his chair to face the kitchen. "Victory, come here."

Paralyzed where she was, she wiped down the appliances and countertops. No response to his words.

"Victory."

Her eyes locked with his. "Huh?"

"Come here."

She dragged herself into the dining room, and took her seat beside him. He grabbed the seat of the chair, and pulled her closer.

"Tell me what's going on."

Focused on her short nails instead of him, she spoke. "Nothing. I just thought you could sleep over like you used to."

"Are you scared to be here alone?"

"No. I just..." She fumbled over her words. "...I just didn't feel like being alone."

"So, you thought what? Let me screw with Mikey?" He rose from his seat, and stalked toward the front door. "I know you said you'd explain things to me later, but where's your fiancé? Why isn't he here? Why isn't he helping you? Why are you back?"

"Wait, Mikey. No. I wasn't trying to screw around with you." She couldn't hide it anymore. The loneliness she felt took over, and she slumped in her chair. "I just wanted a friend around. And I don't have a fiancé. Not anymore. Not since I left my job, and decided to come back here."

"When did all of this happen?"

"Slowly, for months. My bosses made changes within the company. Eventually, they came to me with demands for my department, but I disagreed and attempted to negotiate with them."

"So, what happened?"

"Nothing satisfied them. I decided to take a severance package to save the jobs of my employees, and well...my fiancé wasn't too happy about that."

"So, he left you..."

"No, we made the decision together. He's supposed to sell the house, and send me a check, but until that happens...I need everything..."—she glanced around the house—"...I probably shouldn't have spent what little I did, but...it's hard to be back here."

He walked back to where he left her and knelt in front of

her. "I know it's hard to be here. You should've said something before. I just assumed...you could've called me then, and now. You didn't have to wait for me to show up."

"I didn't want to bother you. I know you have your own life." Her finger ran across the tabletop. "I noticed all of the playthings at your house. For a child. A little girl?"

"Yes. My daughter—Paige."

With a quizzical stare, she turned to him. "Paige. That's a beautiful name. How old is she?"

"Six, but she'd swear she was older." The picture he showed her curved, bent from the shape of his butt.

"She's beautiful. Her hair is just as curly as yours."

"Thank you."

She slid a finger across the picture of the cherub faced little girl, but she no longer saw Paige, tears pooled in her eyes as she began to picture what their child would have looked like. Would their son or daughter resemble Paige? The mix of their hair textures, complexions, heights... What or who would their baby look like?

"Victory."

"Sorry." *Who did Paige look like?* She had his hair, but the rest must be her mother. "Her smile and those eyes. She reminds me of someone." Mikey waited as she flipped the pages of her memory searching for clues to Paige's mother. The tears that were waiting...fell. Not all of them, but some of them. They fell because of loss, pain, and regret. "Rebecca. Rebecca Conley."

He confirmed. "Rebecca is her mother."

Her brows furrowed, and her lips pursed. He took a step

toward her, but her crossed arms and the way she leaned back told him to stay away.

"Rebecca's her mother?"

"Yes."

She looked at him without a word, and sat on the couch. She scratched at her temple with a finger. "Why didn't you tell me earlier?"

"It didn't come up. We hadn't spoken 'til the night I saw you on 240."

"But..." she didn't finish her sentence.

He sat beside her. "But, you left, and you never called. You wouldn't accept my calls."

"I understand. You don't owe me any explanations."

"You understand? I barely have it figured out...there's a lot you don't know."

Before he saw the look in her eyes, he hadn't realized how much he still wanted to resolve the issues in their past. For a long time, he was as angry as she was, but not anymore. The day he saw her on the highway, it all disappeared. And over the past few days, the hollowness inside of him had lost some of its power.

"Now that you've brought my stuff back, I can get Gramps this week. Tomorrow. So, maybe I should go to bed after all."

Damn. That didn't go well. "So, you want me to leave."

"I don't want to intrude. You've probably got to work. And me...I've got so much crap going on right now, I can barely think straight."

"Victory..." He wanted to say something else, but tonight she wasn't going to listen. He rose and walked to the front door.

"Chad...I'm sorry for everything."

The sound of his proper name stopped him at the door. *Chad.* Hand on the knob, he waited for her to finish.

"Thank you for listening...for all of your help."

Sweet Victory

She'd only been back in his life for how many days, and already more barriers had sprung up instead of disappearing. *She'd* left him. Did she expect his life to be on hold? Hers hadn't been.

The end of the week came fast. Victoria plodded through the hallways of the retirement home, The Overlook. A retirement home for the wealthy fifty-five and over. Perched prominently in Memphis' high-rent downtown community, the rooms boasted of some of the best views of the Mississippi. Thank God you couldn't smell the stench of the river. Instead, an odd mixture of paint from the nearby arts center mingled with roast beef from the small bistro where several residents and their visitors laughed over iced teas and lemonades.

As she neared her destination, laughter floated through closed apartment doors. A young girl ran circles around an older gray haired woman as she clapped and sang out on the terrace.

Her stomach lurched, and she leaned a shoulder against a nearby wall. Twelve years of phone calls, and gifts sent via FedEx. But, no visits. Her grandmother's death wasn't his fault, but she missed her, every day. And for some reason, she couldn't separate the two in her mind.

It had taken forever to get past the staff in The Great Room. They didn't know her, and made her sign a million forms and produce ID before she entered.

A soft knock on the solid wood door produced no response. Again, she knocked and waited.

"Come in."

She twisted the knob, and pushed the door open. Inch by inch. A toe entered first, then her head as she peeped around the half-closed door. A quick scan of the small studio. Hanford James, seventy-six, sat in a small wood-framed chair with his back to her. Something on the horizon must have captured his attention. He didn't turn around to see who entered.

"Hello, Victoria."

She tripped over her own foot. He knew it was her. "Grandfather."

"It's time to go?"

Frozen to the floor beside the dinette table, she didn't know what to do. Sit or stand. She remained standing. "Yes, sir." She scanned the muted colored room. Framed watercolor flowers. Small kitchenette, dresser, bed. A picture of her on a table beside his chair. None of the furniture was his. He hadn't wanted any of the furniture from the house. Except for the picture of her and the kitchenette, it reminded her of her college dorm room. "Sir, do you have any bags?" How had he lived in this small room for so long? She'd wanted to get him a two bedroom. She'd planned on visiting, frequently. He didn't think it made sense to spend all of his wife's insurance money on a fancy retirement home, when she'd wanted Victoria to go to college. Besides, when she visited she could sleep on the sofa bed.

A full head of gray hair nodded at two small bags on the other side of the door.

"I'll run them down to the car, and come back for you."

The thin man turned to look at her. "I can walk." Pale wobbly arms pushed a small frame up from the chair. She hadn't noticed before, but he wore his Sunday best: black suit, white shirt, and black tie. It was the same outfit he wore on the day she dropped him off twelve years ago.

He swiped the picture and his hat from the table, and then with slow strides, he shuffled over to where she stood. "Let's go." A crowd of residents, staff, and visitors had gathered in the hall outside of his door. He doled out hugs like a celebrity. "Don't worry, I'll come back to visit."

Someone responded. Female. "You better."

"Mr. James, I'll miss you," a small boy wrapped his arms around her grandfather's hips with such force he teetered.

A kiss and a tussle of the boy's hair, and the small child cried.

"All right, none of that. I'll see you all again. Now, I've got to get home with my granddaughter, Victoria. Isn't she a beautiful young woman?"

Nods accompanied various voices in agreement.

"Come on Victoria, let's go back home."

A slow exit, followed by an even slower car ride across town brought them to their front door later than she'd hoped. With her fingers clinched around the steering wheel, she stared at the small modest brick home with its simple wood frame. How could it compare with the place he'd called home for the last twelve years? Even if it had been their home before that.

After situating her grandfather in his old room, she burst into the kitchen to check the lamb stew in the crockpot. With a wooden spoon, she shoved around potatoes, onions, carrots, peas and turnips. Fanning the wonderfully scented smoke toward her face, she inhaled. "Mmm, heavenly." Her eyes closed, and she took another deep breath.

"Victoria, what smells so good?" She hadn't heard him wander into the kitchen. A smile crossed his face. The twinkle reached his hazel eyes. Eyes that matched hers. "Lamb stew?"

He was quicker than she thought he'd be. The hat, tie and suit jacket were gone, but the suspenders and slacks were still in place. Buffed shoes had been replaced with well-worn house slippers. She searched the drawer for a small spoon; scooped up a bite of stew, and walked toward him. His smile broadened. His hand covered hers as she fed him. " Delicious."

"I'm glad you like it. We can sit and eat if you're ready."

He glanced out of the windows over the sink. "Is it too early for you?"

She waved him off. "No. The staff told me what the normal daily routine was. I don't want to get you off your schedule."

"Don't worry." He ambled over to the dining room table.

Stew, iced tea, yeast rolls, and butter.

Her grandfather scooped up a heaping spoonful of stew, and blew. After a moment, the spoon's contents disappeared. "Victoria, this reminds me of your grandmother's stew."

"Thank you. I tried to remember what she put in hers."

His expression darkened. "I gave you her recipes. What did you do with them?"

Heat flooded her cheeks. "I left them here."

"Here in this house. For twelve years? Where?"

"Yes, sir. I put them in the attic."

His back stiffened, and he put his fork down on the table.

"Those recipes were important to her. I thought she was important to you."

She was. "I just couldn't..."—her words broke off—"...it hurt too much."

His body softened. "Please, promise me you'll check to see if they're still there."

She stared into her bowl of soup. "Yes, sir." God, she

Sweet Victory

was disappointing him already.

"Victoria."

"Yes, sir." She ventured a look.

"I know you blame me."

Again, her eyes lowered. "No, sir."

"Victoria, I'm an old man. You shouldn't lie to me."

"No, sir."

"It was an accident." His voice quivered. Watery hazel eyes sparkled behind out of date glasses. "I was asleep." Pale hands littered with splotchy brown age spots rose to cover his eyes.

She knew he didn't hurt her grandmother. While he slept, she wandered into the kitchen. Dementia. "Yes, sir." Guilt stole her appetite.

His body heaved with a heavy sign. "I've lost my appetite. I think I'm going to go to bed. Thank you for dinner."

He rose from the table and shuffled past her. She spun around in her chair. "Are you sure? I bought a few wrestling DVDs. I know they're your favorite." Suddenly, an urgent need arose within her. Her grandfather's unsteady gait and overly thin physique worried her. One of the two people who'd raised her was gone, and the knot in her chest told her she was quickly becoming anxious about her grandfather. Twelve years gone, wasted. She wanted them back.

Chapter Four

Victoria tugged on the chord dangling from the exposed light above her head. Nothing. Afternoon light streamed in through the round attic window. Cobwebs snared her head; she swiped and squinted. Crowded into a distant corner were boxes containing eighteen years of laugher, love and tears.

She stared across the attic and out the small window at the towering pecan tree. How many times had she wanted to chop it down? She still could hear her grandmother saying, "Go get me a switch." The most brittle piece of wood she could find was her choice on several occasions, but her grandmother used them anyway.

Discipline. Grandma didn't think a child could be raised without it. She guessed her mother didn't like discipline which was why she left home as soon as she could, but she should have stayed. Anytime Grandma punished her, she always told her she loved her, and it was for her own good. And mysteriously, a chocolate cake with pecans, sweet potato pie, peach cobbler or something would appear in the kitchen. And Gramps always sneaked a piece into her bedroom.

Missing and uneven planks caught her sneakers as she stumbled her way across the attic. Once close enough, she sank to her knees. The dusty old floor boards creaked under her weight. Puffs of exposed insulation and dust floated into

Sweet Victory

the air, tickling her nose. "Achoo," she sniffed. She wiped at the dust-covered boxes. Her handwriting in black marker began to peek through. "Halloween, Christmas, Gramps, Grandma." She'd take the two marked Gramps and Grandma. She kept searching. There were some she didn't recognize. The handwriting didn't look like hers either. One read, College. The other, Victory. She decided to take them downstairs, too.

She stacked two of the boxes on top of each other, and then the other two in the same manner. With caution, she pushed the two stacks toward the entrance of the attic. At the ladder, she changed her position. Lifting a leg to step over the boxes, she placed it back down awkwardly straddling the stacks. Shifting her feet in an effort to get in front of the boxes, the heel of her sneaker sank into the soft insulation. She lost her balance. Her hands searched for something stabilizing: the boxes, the floorboards around the attic's opening. The only thing she caught were the boxes she'd tugged to the edge of the attic's opening, which plummeted down after her as she tumbled and slipped down the rickety ladder.

Thump. Crack. Her butt smacked against one of her new decorative tables. A dull shooting pain flashed through her backside. "Victoria, what the..."—the words cut off as she fell into his arms—"...what were you thinking?"

She gazed up into Chad's brown eyes. Maybe it was her imagination, but they seemed a little darker. His eyebrows were pinched together in a familiar crease she recalled so well from their childhood. He helped her stand and surveyed the area. The boxes she'd carefully stacked were strewn across the floor, the contents no longer hidden away.

He let go of her, and walked to one of the boxes that had landed near a table. "Why did you try to pull all of these boxes down by yourself? You should've moved them one by one, or called if you needed help."

Her grandfather snacked on a bag of his favorite pork skins as he stood in his bedroom doorway watching. The bag rose to hide a slight upturn of his lips as he munched, leaning against the doorframe and watching.

"Gramps wanted me to pull down Grandma's recipes." She knelt down, and began to gather up some of the books and papers.

Chad finished collecting the papers where he stood, slid the box into a corner, and then he strolled over to her. "Why'd you try to move so many at one time?"

She focused on her papers, and tried to avoid the distraction of his eyes. "I didn't mean to. I saw a few boxes I didn't recognize, and decided to bring them down, too."

He kneeled beside her. "Well, how about we sort through some of this together, and then, put what you don't need back in the attic?"

"Chad, I don't want to be any sort of burden for you. You don't have to babysit me." She glanced around the room at the mess she'd made. Goodness. Again, he'd come to her rescue. The fall from the attic could've broken a leg or worse. "Thank you again, but you've got other things to worry about. You don't need me clouding up your life."

"You're not clouding up my life in any way..."—he set the papers in his hand down, and placed one hand on each of her shoulders. He spun her to face him. "I'm happy you're back." He paused. "I'm sorry you found out about Rebecca and Paige the way you did, but I tried to tell you."

That confused her. "You tried to tell me. When? How?"

"Phone calls, letters. Once, I even..." He didn't finish.

"Once you what?"

"It doesn't matter, the point is I tried, but after a while..."—he glanced at the box in the corner. She made a

49

mental note to check that freaking box.   "...after a while I gave up."

"Children, are you both going to squat and squabble in the middle of the room all day or are we going to get something to eat?"   Gramps stood over them with a devilish grin.

Victoria's head swiveled back and forth between her grandfather, and Chad.   "By the way, Chad, what are you doing here?"

"I invited him for lunch.   It's boring hanging out with you all day.   You don't do anything but lay around on the couch watching that dang television."   After dropping a bombshell about her dull life on Chad, he sauntered back into his room.   "Chad, those boxes you stuck up in the attic for me, make sure they're okay."

In a blink a frown crossed Chad's face.   Those boxes held answers to questions she hadn't known she had.

"Yes, sir."

"What did you do for my Gramps?"

"Nothing really, when I visited him he'd always give me something you'd sent that he wanted stored.   So, I put it all up in the attic."

"I thought the management company had someone renting this place out."

"For a while.   Me."

What?   Why didn't she know *that*?   "You stayed here?"

"For a few years right after high school.   I needed a place, and Gramps wouldn't hear of it otherwise."

"Why?   What was going on?"

His head shook back and forth.   "Nothing.   Just had some things to work out."

As they tucked the last few pieces of papers back into their box, she watched a shadow darken his expression.

"Oh."

"Anyway, your Gramps wants lunch.   What do you suggest?"

The box beneath her fingertips held a lot of possibilities.   She tapped at the box.   With each tap, her body tingled. "Let's find something from here."

"I think he'd like that a lot."

Chad carried the box to the dining room table, and placed it on one of the chairs.   The books and papers they'd just placed inside, they spread across the table.   "Would you like anything to drink?"

"Iced tea."

By the time she'd returned from the kitchen with two glasses of iced tea, he'd already begun to categorize the items from the boxes.   A few piles sat on the table in front of her.

"I didn't know how you'd like to begin, so I put them in piles of desserts, chicken, beef, and etcetera."

"That's great."   She placed coasters on the table, and sat the teas on them.   "You keep doing that, and I'll look through the piles to see if I can break them out further, and find something for lunch."

Yellowed pieces of paper, smeared and dingy from age, with her grandmother's familiar handwriting, trembled in her hands.   She grabbed for, but missed fragile pieces that crumbled to the floor.   For so many years, she'd tried to forget.   To forget her scent, her voice...her face. *Why?* As she stared blankly at a recipe for an okra, tomato and corn stew, images she'd pushed away rushed back.   Pages slipped from her hand to the table.   She caught the table's edge with her hands, and breathed.   Short quick breaths.   An ache in her stomach traveled to her chest, and her breathing became an uneasy wheeze.   Sweat beaded on the backs of her hands, as her grip tightened on the table.

A cool wet hand trailed across her forehead, and through her hair.   A bowl of water appeared on the table beside her, and Chad's long, strong fingers dipped into the water, cupping a small amount in his palms.   "Victory, dip your head."   She couldn't move.   The water poured from his hands back into the bowl.   His damp palms patted her cheeks and forehead.   The feel of his fingers on her skin calmed and soothed.   The sweat on the back of her hands disappeared, but the fire inside of her moved from her chest, and took over her whole body.

She leaned her body into his feeling his solid chest press against her back.   His hands smoothed up and down her arms, then wrapped around her waist.   The stubble along his jaw-line rubbed her cheek.   Gently, his hand tilted her face so her eyes met his.   His lips caressed hers.   Not overpowering.   Not overwhelming.   Tender.

He stared into her eyes.   Searching for something.   As she prepared to ask, his mouth covered hers.   This time, his kiss was not as gentle.   She angled her neck to give him better access.   He tasted her, and she him.   With her eyes closed, she felt all of him.   His chest.   His hands.   His thighs pressed against hers.   His mouth was sinful.   It awakened things in her she'd pushed away even before she left Corey. She and Corey hadn't been intimate for months before she left.   Work was always more important, for him.

Her body pressed into Chad's, and his responded.   The bulge in his pants pushed against her bottom.   Reality set in. Her eyes sprang open, and she pulled away; crushing her body against the nearest cold wall.   "Chad."   She leaned out from the wall, and scanned for her grandfather.   Nowhere to be seen, now, but then her eyes were closed.   "Did Gramps see us?"

Panting, Chad leaned against the table.   "I don't know.

Maybe..."

She didn't know what she wanted to say. "Maybe?"

The look on his face morphed from pleasure to uncertainty.

Gramps strolled in with the same bag of skins. "Have you two figured out anything, yet?"

Her face heated in shame. How could she stand in the dining room, and be mauled while her grandfather was in the other room?

"Nawh, Gramps, we haven't found anything, yet. Do you have anything in particular you want?"

"No, I'll let you two kids decide." He turned. "Yell when you two are ready." And he was gone as quickly as he'd come.

Hours later, her grandfather sat at the head of the dining room table, while she sat at his side staring into Chad's eyes. The chair at the other end of the table was empty. She watched as her grandfather attempted to avoid resting his eyes on the empty chair. Chad reached across the table and grabbed her hand. The touch of his skin against hers combined with the softness of his gaze brought back memories of their high school romance. When they were young her grandmother would spend the day in the kitchen preparing something special for them. She focused on the kitchen door behind Chad wishing her grandmother would walk through it at any minute with a casserole dish or a fresh pitcher of tea.

Although she tried to erase some of the sadness in the house with new furniture and appliances, she remembered everything with each moment she stood in her

Sweet Victory

grandmother's kitchen. Her grandmother's voice echoed in her ear. "Don't make the fried green tomatoes too thin. Sweetie, those are some pretty pieces of fried catfish. Perfect with some sweet cornbread, and collard greens."

With each slice and dip of tomato or fish, her troubles with money and jobs faded away. Each stir of the cornbread batter calmed her. Her grandmother would probably frown at the turkey necks in the greens instead of hammocks. For the first time in weeks, she did not feel like sleeping away the day or turning off her phone to avoid bill collectors.

For dessert, she planned on surprising Gramps with a coconut pineapple upside down cake. She'd also made some candies: chocolate covered coconut with almonds. As a child, her grandmother used to let her make each little chocolate ball by hand. As they cooled, her fingerprints would dry into the chocolate. Her grandmother always called them *Sweet Victory*.

A soft squeeze of her other hand by her grandfather directed her attention back to the table; she realized both men were holding her hands and waiting. Waiting for her to rejoin them.

Gramps spoke. "Victory, this food is delicious. Your grandmother would be so proud."

"Thanks Gramps. Grandma's old recipes were in really good shape. I think I'm going to type them into my computer, and take the originals and laminate them or something."

"This cornbread is awesome. It's sweet, but not too sweet." Chad removed his hand from hers, and broke his cornbread apart. "What's inside of it?"

She'd changed her grandma's cornbread a teeny bit. "It's pineapple. You really like it?" She held her breath waiting.

Chad slipped a small piece of bread into her mouth,

and then his. This time, adding a lick of his fingertips. "I love it."

Gramps put his hand to his mouth, and coughed. "Me, too, sweetie."

After dinner, she cleared away the dishes, and disappeared into the kitchen. The cake was hidden beneath an old cake pan of her grandma's, and the candies were arranged on an old plate.

The sweet smell of pineapple wafted through the air when the cake pan touched the table. "Guys don't touch anything." The smile on Gramps' face warmed her heart. She vanished into the kitchen, and returned with the plate of candies.

"Victory, are those the coconut candies we used to steal from the fridge as kids?" Chad's stare bounced between the candies and her.

"Yep. Remember how Grandma would chase us out of the kitchen?"

"How could I forget?" He reached out to grab a candy, and she slapped his hand. "What?"

"I've got to give Gramps his surprise first." She removed the top of the cake pan, and her grandfather's eyes grew wide. The smell of pineapple and coconut mingled with chocolate, and filled the small area. A hearty slice for Gramps, and a small piece for herself. Then she loaded chocolate candies on another plate for Chad, and a couple on her own. She poured everyone a cup of coffee and sat.

"Victory, this is delicious."

"Thanks, Gramps."

"You know sweetie, you should open a restaurant."

"What?"

"You know Victory, that's not a bad idea," said Chad.

Sweet Victory

"Please you two. I don't have the money or the time. I've got to find another job." Because of Chad, she hadn't lost much with her move to Tennessee, but she needed to be able to take care of herself and Gramps, and her nest egg wouldn't last forever.

"Think about it Victory, this could *be* your new job. You love cooking. You could start small, and grow slowly."

"Listen gentlemen, I don't know anything about restaurants, and I cook for fun, for ya'll, not for profit."

The two men exchanged glances, but no words. "Okay, sweetie," said Gramps.

"Thanks Gramps."

"We'll talk about it later." Her grandfather sat quietly and sipped his cup of coffee.

"Sure, Gramps, sure."

Chapter Five

A day hadn't passed since that dinner that Gramps or Chad hadn't mentioned Victoria's cooking, her grandmother's recipes or her turning it all into some type of business. Mysteriously, her laptop would have the Small Business Development Center homepage loaded. Recipe books would pop up with sticky notes about how her version of the same dish looked and probably tasted better.

She had to admit although she hadn't thought about it before it would be great to have her own business, and she did love to cook, especially since her grandmother passed away. The scent of fresh basil, garlic, and onion reminded her of her grandmother; temporarily easing her mind, and allowing her to forget about everything going on around her. Every slice, chop or mix of an ingredient was therapeutic. Corey had never cared for her cooking. Tiny food on large plates for unreasonable amounts of money at the latest *in* spot suited him more.

Along with using her grandmother's recipes, she'd be able to control the hiring and firing. The budgets. The direction and growth of the company. What could it hurt? She could at least take a look around the SBDC website. Her grandmother had always been a strong woman. Sometimes too powerful—controlling. But, she'd always been a woman in charge of her own path. Something, that recently, Victoria had given up.

Sweet Victory

Sinking deeper into the couch cushions, she pulled her laptop on her thighs, and hit the power button. After a few simple keystrokes, she'd found what she was searching for. The SBDC offered loans to help with startup. There was an office on Beale Street. With a click of the bookmark tab, she decided to go and speak with them to see what they could help her do.

Fantasies assuaged for a moment, she clicked onto her favorite job search website, and typed in her password. Nothing interesting. Sales clerk. Insurance salesperson. How many insurance companies where there in the world? All of them had positions open, and one by one they were contacting her. It annoyed her each time one of them called to say "Hello, Ms. James, I work for a fortune 500 company. We've reviewed your resume, and believe you would be a great fit for us." They never said who they represented, and her hopes were always dashed out when she returned their call. She didn't want to sell insurance; she just wanted a job in her field. Take care of her grandfather. Pay their bills. But, maybe having her own business could do all of that and give her more.

After an unsuccessful hour of job searching, and another unproductive thirty minutes talking with recruiters, she went back to the SBDC website. With each tap of the keys, she remembered her grandmother's words. "Whatcha gonna do, now? Give up?" When she last heard those words, she was eighteen years old, and pregnant. Her grandmother made it clear she'd have to finish school, and go to college whether she had the baby or not. "James women aren't weak. We don't give up." But, if she had the baby, she wouldn't be able to attend the college she wanted. Scholarship money would disappear, and she would not be able to cheer her first year. "Baby, whatever you decide, you have us. But, you have got to make a decision."

She made her decision, took action, and *then* she told Mikey. A chill flowed through her at the memory. The mistakes in her past were all haunting her. Why was he so kind to her even now? Why come to her aid after she'd betrayed him? The ghostly words of her grandmother would not go away. "Baby, make a decision." The money she had in her savings wouldn't last forever. To forget Mikey, she ran to DC. To forget DC, she ran to Tennessee. *James women aren't weak.* No more giving in, up, or running. She made an appointment.

With her portfolio in hand, Victoria stepped out of her car onto Beale Street. The introductory entrepreneurial class offered by the SBDC was tucked away in an older building in the industrial part of North Memphis. Working and non-working factories surrounded her, silently judging her decision to start her own business.

The online survey she'd taken prior to signing up for the class seemed to question her decision as much as she did. She had no idea how to answer most of the questions. Do people see you as a leader? Do you know where to go to get an EIN? Do you know if you need to have intellectual property insurance? What on earth? She had no idea. The free seminar, she hoped, would get her started.

The conference room was filled with more people than Victoria expected. As the people in the room introduced themselves, and spoke about their backgrounds, she knew why. So many of them were like her. Because of the economy, they'd been laid off, fired, or found themselves in various states of underemployment. Instead of sitting around, they'd decided to use what little funds they had to do something.

By the time the class was over, Victoria floated back to

her car. She had signed up for the next class. It wasn't free, but she could afford the twenty dollars. It would help her with marketing her idea, selling desserts and sweets over the Internet. The SBDC sponsored a business plan competition. A $2,500 prize would be awarded to the winner. If nothing else, it would be able to help her with the build-out of her website. Of course, she had to participate, and win. And she wasn't sure about that part, yet.

She couldn't wait to tell Chad and her grandfather about the class.

When Victoria arrived home, her Gramps was sleeping. She stripped off her suit and heels, and pulled on her most comfortable sweats. Although she needed a computer desk, she hadn't bought one. So, she set up her laptop on the dining room table, and placed all of her papers from the class on the table beside it.

As she sat, something caught her eye. The boxes from the attic. She had forgotten all about them. Tucked between the buffet and the wall nearly covered by the drapes, she wouldn't have noticed them if she'd sat in a different seat.

The legs of her chair scuffed the floor as she pushed back. This time, she brought the boxes over to the table one by one. The first box she opened was filled with letters she'd sent her grandfather. There were a few pictures, too. Pictures of her and friends from college. Some of the people in the pictures she hadn't thought about in quite some time. There was even a picture of her and Corey.

She read through a few of the letters. They sounded so cold. So empty. As she thought of her sleeping grandfather in the bedroom down the hall, she couldn't understand why the letters were so distant. He'd needed her as much as she'd needed him. She wouldn't make the same mistake again. No matter what, she'd always take care of him.

She made the decision to scrapbook some of the items

in the box as a surprise for her grandfather. In one photo, she wore a red and white dress with her grandmother hugging her from behind. They both had huge bubble gum smiles, and afros. She ran her fingers through her curly hair, and wondered how an afro was possible, but there it was staring back at her. Her grandmother's bronzed complexion juxtaposed against jet black hair jumped off the picture. Being raised by an iron-fisted grandmother was hard, but grandma had lost her only daughter to a man, and drugs.

High on drugs, Victoria's father had beaten her mother in the bathroom of their apartment. The police showed up at her grandparents' house with a scared young Victoria. She'd never left because her mother had never awakened. A lioness protecting her cub was the only way to describe her childhood with her grandmother. No one dared cause her any pain, and she never got out of line. Until Mikey. He'd been worth any risk. Sometimes she feared her father would come back, and take her, but he disappeared into the Memphis judicial system.

The smiling woman in the picture had loved, protected, and nurtured her for her entire life. Warm tears flowed down her cheeks. Salt tingled her tongue as she ran it across her lips. With the back of her hand, she dabbed at her cheeks. Some of the pictures could be framed and placed around the house, but this one might be perfect for her website.

She now knew what she would name her desserts. Sweet Victory. It was perfect. She set a few of the other photos to the side. The rest of the items she placed back inside the box before grabbing the next one.

This box wasn't her grandfather's or her grandmother's.

It was Chad's.

Letters he'd written. Letters she'd returned. Letters he'd never mailed. Pictures of them as kids. Pictures of

61

him and her grandfather in the retirement home. The home she never visited. In her absence, Chad had become the grandchild she couldn't bear to be.

Each letter she read reminded her of why she'd originally left Memphis. Chad and Rebecca. Rebecca Conley had been co-captain of the cheerleading squad. Victoria had been captain. Rebecca always wrapped herself around Chad, varsity basketball player, every chance she got.

At the end of senior year after a big win at an away game they'd all sneaked some liquor back to their hotel rooms. Rebecca and Chad hooked up. Victoria had no reason to be jealous. Convincing herself of this was easier when she was eighteen.

Chad had been her first, and she'd been his. He'd waited for her after practice one day to drive her home. It'd been raining, and they drove with the windows down. Rain blew sideways into the car, and every street they turned onto smelled of wet earth and honeysuckle. The sky above was gray, but not sad. Instead of going straight to her grandparent's house, they went to his house to pick up a movie to watch.

When he dropped her at home, her grandparents weren't there. A simple touch of his hand dusting rain from her hair turned into an afternoon of the two of them learning each other in ways she had never thought about. The feel of his hand on her skin had awakened all of her senses. He had fumbled with her zippers, and her with his buttons, but they both figured it out. Gentle and slow, he took his time, and made sure she was comfortable, but she'd wanted him so much she didn't allow him to get protection.

God. Freaking tears wouldn't stop. They dripped all over the pictures she held in her hands. She surveyed everything around her. All of the sadness, and loss had been her fault. *Hers.* All of these years, she had hidden away to avoid facing the truth. Mikey and her Gramps reminded her of pain she wanted to forget.

The week after that game, conversations ended every time Victoria entered a classroom. Rebecca had spread word she and Chad were an item, and Victoria was so jealous, she'd tried to get her kicked off the squad. Some of the squad backed Victoria up, but not enough, and Rebecca continued to spread lie after lie. None of them were true, but their coach and teachers believed Rebecca. Victoria had fallen into a weird no-friend zone. Gone from being popular cheerleader to eating alone outside.

In the flash of a high school minute, Rebecca replaced her as captain. Her scholarships for cheering were gone. She was lucky. Just as many colleges had offered her academic scholarships. The further away the better, a college in the nation's capital, she took it.

When she left, rumor had it Rebecca was pregnant. Obviously, it hadn't been true, but eventually she got what she wanted—Paige, their child.

The letters she read, twelve years later at her table explained everything. He had been led to believe there was a baby. Their parents had wanted them to get married, but he refused. As a result, his parents had cut him off, but later they discovered Rebecca had lied again. That's why Gramps had let him live in the home for a few years...without paying a dime. He didn't have any other place to go. He'd written about the possibility of moving to DC with her, but she didn't know since she didn't read his mail. Marked in red on envelope after envelope were the words Return to Sender, scribbled in her own handwriting.

She'd just assumed all of the letters had her grandparents' address on them because he was trying to be sentimental. Remind her of where they made love. Unknowingly, remind her of their child.

As she folded the last letter to place it back into its envelope, her grandfather ambled into the room. "Hey baby." His cheery voice helped to remove her sadness.

She wiped at the dried tears on her face. "Hey Granddaddy. Are you hungry?"

He pulled out a chair and sat at the table beside her. "Sure am." He peeked at the envelope in her hand. "What ya reading?"

"Nothing. Just looking through the boxes. I found some old pictures and stuff." She motioned toward the items lying on the table in front of her. "Would you mind if I put these into picture frames?"

His frail fingers poked at the pictures shuffling them around on the table. "These old things. Are you sure?" An expression somewhere between joy and wonder crossed his face.

"Yes sir. I love these old pictures." She scanned the room. There was new paint and furniture, but no art or anything, yet. "It's pretty bare in here."

"Great. Where do you want to put them?"

"Well, maybe we can blow a few of them up, and put them on the walls, the others I thought maybe we could place around the living room and den."

"Sounds good."

"Perfect. I'll work on it." She stood and walked towards the kitchen. "So, what would you like for dinner?"

His eyes glazed over as he rubbed his stomach. "Uhh, how about smothered chicken. Smothered chicken and rice."

Goodness, her grandfather would eat some form of chicken and rice everyday if she allowed him. "Are you sure Granddaddy? We just had that the other day."

The shine in his eyes dimmed a little. "Well, if you'd like something else."

She shook her head. "Oh, no. I just thought maybe you were tired of it."

"Nawh, baby. Your grandmother used to make it for me all of the time." His eyes drifted back down to one of the pictures on the table. "In the retirement, home theirs didn't taste anything like hers. And it couldn't hold a candle to yours." He rose from the table and joined her in the kitchen. A soft kiss on her cheek made her heart thud. "You could make that for me every day, and I would love it."

"Okay. Chicken and rice it is." She'd forgotten how much they used to eat chicken and rice when she was a kid. Some nights she and her grandmother would eat something completely different, but he would have his chicken and rice. "Granddaddy, I forgot to tell you. I went to the small business development center..."

"Tell me what happened. When do we start making desserts?"

"How'd you know?"

"Who do you think takes your laptop off of you, and covers you up when you fall asleep on the couch?" His smile said it all. He was happy for her. Proud of her.

"Well, it's only the beginning. I've got a lot to do."

"I'll help. I can't cook..." —he rubbed his stomach— "...but, I can definitely taste anything. Just to make sure everything is okay." He grinned.

"Perfect." She grabbed some chicken out of the freezer, and a cast iron skillet from a cabinet. "Don't tell Chad. Okay? I want to surprise him."

He winked. "It will be our secret."

Chapter Six

The proof of the ad stared at Victoria. Friday, Saturday, and Sunday, plus the ad would run simultaneously on The Commercial Appeal's website. Simple straight forward copy in black summed up one of the most *important* things in her life. A picture of Corey clutching his heart, and gasping as he fell backwards onto a chair in the living room flashed in her mind. He would never understand her decision, but it was ridiculous for her to drive around in an $80,000 car when she and Gramps needed money.

2008 Black Lexus LX 570

27,320 miles

$50,000 or best offer

Call V. James 901.555.1234

The last line took the price from $51 to $76. And she had no idea how many times she would need to run the ad. The car was unnecessary. The money from the car could be used to pay for licensing, liability insurance, packager/distributor fees—so many things—and she wouldn't have to worry about dipping into the money she and her grandfather were living off.

Without a job, applying for small business loans based on the merit of her business plan had gone nowhere. But with money from the sale of her car, and credit cards—at least the ones she still had, she could do it. Still, it would be tricky. The most significant cost would be rental of a licensed facility to produce, package, and store product. With a small amount of orders, she'd be able to cover the cost of the charges against her credit cards until orders increased.

The key would be pre-orders. How would she get those?

Her response to the email proof was one word. *Approved.*

She sighed at the ringing of the phone on the end table. *Bill collectors.* They were her first call in the morning and the last call at night, most nights. She'd turned the ringer off the phone in her bedroom because they woke her every morning, and that's when she did sleep. She checked the caller ID. Chad. "Hello." All day, she'd hoped he'd call. Even though she'd spoken with him earlier that morning, she still missed his presence.

"Hey, how are you doing?"

"I just finalized the ad."

His voice softened. "You sure you want to sell the car?"

"Yeah, I just need something big enough for me and Gramps with a smaller price tag. Maybe big enough to carry around a few things for the business." Honestly, it wasn't difficult to sell it. It was more about what it represented. Her and Corey. Her life in D.C.

She swore she heard a sigh of relief in his voice. "Well, there are a lot of great cars you can buy from the police auctions. They'll cost you almost nothing."

"Really? Are you serious?" Old police cars? "What kind of cars?"

"They are usually cars seized for different reasons: drug seizures, police cars with high mileage, fire department cruisers."

"So, would they need repairing or anything?"

"That's why you have me."

Every time he joked with those words, she hoped. The letters filling the box tucked away in her room should have been responded to years ago. If so, she probably would've had a chance, but why would he truly trust her again when she left him? "What would I do without you?"

"I don't plan on letting you find out again."

The words had so much promise. She didn't know what to say. Should she mention the old letters—the fact she realized cutting him out of her life had been a huge mistake. "Could we take a look at some of the cars soon? That way I wouldn't have to put any extra miles on the car. Maybe I'll be able to get more money."

"You could use my car, and I'll ride my motorcycle until we find something."

"Motorcycle?" She remembered her first night back in town, he'd approached her on a motorcycle, but she didn't know he had his own, too. "The weather is getting bad. You should keep your car, and I'll get a rental if I have to do a lot of driving."

"You don't need to waste the money. The roads are good, and we haven't been getting much rain."

"Are you sure?" The idea of Mikey hurt because he helped her would drive her mad.

"Victory, it's no big deal. I'll be over later tonight. I have an idea to help you promote the desserts. We'll have to work fast."

The speed with which he changed the subject nearly gave her whiplash. Since she'd come back to Memphis, he'd been doing nothing, but taking care of her. Corey would never give up his Range Rover for her on any day. Once, she'd asked him to use his computer when hers was down to

Sweet Victory

complete a project for work. He said, "No." She'd bought him the computer as a birthday gift. But, being able to depend on Mikey felt natural. If she had to stop again, she didn't know what she'd do. "Why? What is it?"

He chuckled. "Woman, you don't like surprises? I'll be there tonight. And we'll talk about it then. Okay?"

A million things floated into her mind at the sound of his words. Clean-up. Shower. Cook. "Okay, would you like anything special for dinner? You have to let me thank you some way."

"There are a lot of ways you can thank me, Victory." A smoky sound colored his words promising to let her know just how she could thank him.

"Mikey, you need to stop playing around."

Desire replaced the laughter in his voice. "I never said I was joking." The six simple words confused her. "I might be a little late. I've got to drop some stuff off for Paige."

The sound of his daughter's name made her stomach flip. How could she be jealous? Of his child? She'd had the same chance as Rebecca, but she'd given it up. What was he dropping off, and would Rebecca be there, too? Of course, she was the mother of his child. Rebecca would probably answer the door wearing red lingerie with two glasses of wine in her hand.

God, she was going to drive herself crazy.

The doorbell rang. Victoria placed the last dish into the dishwasher. Each chime excited her more. Grabbing the towel hanging from the refrigerator handle, she dried her

70

hands before running them through her hair. All day long, she'd been waiting to see him.

She tossed the dishtowel onto the sink, and headed toward the living room. For some reason, she tripped over nothing, and had to catch herself against the wall beside the door. Her high school reaction to Mikey coming over made her laugh as she opened the door. "Hey."

"What's so funny?"

Uniform. Dark blue. Gun. What else was hanging from that belt? Was that his chest or a bulletproof vest? Did the shoes add height to him or was he always so tall? She wanted to hug him, kiss him. It'd been a long time since they'd *really* kissed, but she remembered every touch of his lips. Goosebumps prickled her skin at the powerful memory.

"Victoria, you gonna answer me or let me in?"

He rested his hand above her hip, and leaned in to kiss her on the cheek. His lips were as gentle as she remembered. She wanted so much more, but maybe it wasn't a good time. She had nothing. What could she offer him? Could he forgive her? *God, she doubted everything.* "I'm sorry, Mikey. I tripped on the way to the door. Come in."

His hand still rested on her hip just above her bottom. The familiar touch of his hand against her body grounded and comforted her. The spot he stroked connected straight to her heart. With each moment, the bond grew stronger. She turned to walk to the couch. His hand slid to the small of her back, but he didn't remove it. Only when he stopped to close the door was the link broken, and she missed it instantly.

He reached into his pocket, and pulled out a wad of folded papers.

"We're going to be a vendor in Memphis in May."

71

Sweet Victory

Okay, what on earth was Mikey thinking? Memphis in May! More than thirty years of history for Memphis. An annual month long celebration of music, food, and all things Memphis. And for fun they threw in an international element tying in a connection with another country. "What? What do we have to do for that?"

"It's all right here." He stripped off his jacket, and spread the pages he held across the table.

Victoria stared at his arms, chest, thighs, and then the pages. "Seriously, Memphis in May. What would we do there?"

Brown eyes filled with confusion blinked. "What do you mean? We're going to sell whatever you have."

She fondled the pages, scanning pictures, and skimming the information. "April. The first event is in April!"

"I know. It's Memphis in May, but the kick-off is the last day in April. But, we've got time. We need to get this form in by mid-February. They'll let us know if we're accepted by the end of February, and then we've got 'til April 30th."

"Do you believe five months is enough time to get licensing, inspections, packaging, and everything else?" Victoria rolled her head from side to side, and gave a little moan. Suddenly, a tightness gripped her between her shoulder blades, and wouldn't go away. She flexed and rotated her shoulders.

Mikey stripped off his shirt. The shirt revealed a Kevlar vest, but she knew his chest was as firm. He disappeared into the kitchen. A moment later, he returned without his gun. He threw the vest on a chair, and untucked his t-shirt before he sat down on the couch, and slipped off his shoes. He kicked a leg up behind her, and rested his back against the arm of the couch. "Turn around."

His thumbs massaged the base of her neck, and then they slid firmly up and down the back of her neck. Gently, he stretched her neck and shoulders. "Mmm." Slowly, his hands slipped down her shoulders caressing her arms, and then back to her shoulders. With a gentle push to the middle of her back, he signaled her to lean forward, and his magical fingers worked each and every knot in her back until they disappeared. But, he replaced her tension with something else, something much more dangerous—desire.

She reached for the papers on the table, wanting to take her mind off his touch. "I would love to do this, but I don't know."

His fingers kneaded stressing each of his words. "Together, we can do this."

"Mmm. God, that feels so good."

"You're tense. Why?"

Because you're touching me. She shook the papers at him. "This and everything else. I guess I have a lot on my mind." She kept reading. "I don't think I realized Memphis in May had four different events."

"That's because the barbeque competition is always blasted everywhere."

"You know we watched..."—she paused, and Mikey's hands stopped for a moment—"...it a few times on The Food Network."

"OK. So, you know it's not something you should miss."

"The Beale Street Music Festival begins on April 30th. The Barbeque competition begins on May 13th, and then the Sunset Symphony is on May 29th. " She sat up twisting around to face him. "Hmm, it sounds like a lot."

"International week is really nothing for us unless you want to try to make a dessert that fits with whatever country

73

they choose.   We can skip the Sunset Symphony, too—people are allowed to bring in their own food.   But, I think last year, something like, 200,000 people attended the music festival and the barbeque competition."

"We have to provide menu, prices, and space requirements."   She ran her finger down one of the pages, as she read.   "There are fees for electrical, health department, code enforcement."

His hands rested on her shoulders.   "Listen Victory, are you going to give up before we even begin?   The first thing we've got to do is fill out the form."   A crooked smile accompanied bright mischievous eyes.   "Who knows, we might not even be chosen.   A committee of four people determines who gets the slots."

"A committee, huh?"

"Yeah."

"Why do you know so much about this?"

His hands dropped from her shoulders, and for a brief moment, his eyes shifted.   "It's called research."   He leaned back against the arm of the couch.   "What's it going to be?"

"So, we've got about two weeks, huh."

Damn that crooked, perfect, smile.

"Yep."

Chapter Seven

A cold gust of air whipped past Victoria's ear as she shut the door. She kicked her shoes into a corner, and dropped her keys on a nearby table.

She fingered the mail beside her keys. "Gramps, is there any other mail?"

Gramps sauntered out of his room with a bowl full of ice cream. "No, just what's there." He pointed at the table. "I made reservations for dinner tonight."

"Awh, Gramps, I'm kind of tired. I've been running all day. First, the photo shoot of the food for the menus, and then I met with the web designer." She plopped onto the couch. "I'm exhausted."

"Sorry, baby, but I've made a reservation, and I can't break it." He turned, and disappeared into his room. "I'm going to take a nap, but be ready by 7:30 P.M."

"Gramps..."

"Nap time."

She sighed in resignation. Apparently, she would not win the argument tonight. Shoeless, she kicked her feet up on the couch, and flicked on the TV. Her eyes would not stay open, so, she decided a nap might not be a bad idea.

A gentle shake of her shoulders woke her. "Victory, get up. Victory."

"Oh God, Gramps. What time is it?"

Sweet Victory

Gramps was decked out in his Sunday best: black suit, hat, and shiny shoes. "It's OK, sweetie. It's only 6:30 P.M."

She sprang up from the cushions. "Gramps, I'll be ready in thirty minutes. Don't worry." The magazines on the table bounced. She grabbed her knee. "Ouch." She limped toward her room.

"Wear that really pretty red dress of yours."

Red dress. She could never wear that red dress out with her grandfather. It would be saved for a date, a night on the town with Mikey. If she wore it tonight people in the restaurant would think she was a gold digger. "No, Gramps, I don't think it's appropriate." She slung the door shut behind, and stripped as she raced toward her bathroom.

His words trailed behind her.

"Wear it. It's beautiful."

A panicked heartbeat later, Victoria twisted the knob on her bedroom door slowly. The reflection she caught in her dresser mirror worried her. The dip in the back of the dress was dangerously close to being indecent, but she'd clipped a broach mid-way down her back to make it more appropriate for an evening with Gramps. Along with a black wrap draped over her shoulders, and her coat, it was perfect. She hurried into the living room where her Grandfather waited patiently.

"Victory." Her grandfather touched the rim of his cap, and then stuck out his arm. "Any man who sees you tonight will fall instantly in love."

She placed a soft kiss on his cheek. "Thanks, Gramps."

Twenty minutes later, they pulled up in front of The Peabody. For a brief moment, they sat in the car. "Gramps, should we really waste money on this. I could cook something for us at home." Gramps exited the car. The valet took her keys, and they walked inside.

"It's all taken care of."

"Gramps, how is it taken care of? We are on a budget. I've blown enough money. But, I didn't think it would take this long to find a job. And I never thought I'd be trying to start my own business. This is all so..."

Gramps rubbed his hand along her arm. "Don't worry, sweetie."

The sound of Victoria's shoes echoed off the marble floors of the grand hallway as she and Gramps walked arm in arm down the main entrance of The Peabody. Vaulted ceilings, wood and glass curios, and old wood fixtures carved and treated with respect and love since 1925.

As a child, Victoria had been told stories of The Peabody. Because her grandparents had fallen in love at a time in the south when everyone did not agree with interracial relationships, The Peabody had been off limits. Although it frustrated her grandfather, it absolutely angered her grandmother, and she decided she'd make her home look as nice, and she could cook as well as any chef The Peabody hired. And in Victoria's opinion, she had.

Gramps guided Victoria through the hallways until they stopped at the grand entrance of Chez Philippe. Brown and white marble columns, murals depicting soldiers and southern belles adorned the walls, gold painted molding, and lavish furnishings welcomed them. A hostess greeted them, and led them to their table. Her breath caught in her throat. Black suit, white shirt, no tie, curly blond locks tamed, Chad stood as she and her gramps approached.

The auburn tint to her hair had begun to fade with the

lack of constant Memphis sun. Black curls kissed the top of her shoulders. As he removed her coat, the scent of lavender perfumed the air. Her bare shoulders called for his kiss. As he slid the coat down her arms, his hands caressed them. Soft skin teased him. "Victoria, you look beautiful."

A quick flash of cinnamon flooded her cheeks. "Thank you."

He turned to Gramps. "And sir, I have to say, I love the suspenders."

Gramps ran his thumbs along his suspenders. "Thank you."

The waitress brought them all drinks. Gramps raised his glass of iced tea to offer a toast. "I think we should toast."

"A toast? To what?" asked Victoria.

"Gramps and I are proud of you and your decision to move forward with the business."

"Yeah," she glanced at Gramps before focusing on Mikey again.

"We know all of this has been scary, but we're all together again. *We* can do it." Mikey added.

"Yes, sweetie, you're back home, and this time you have got to stay with us."

Victoria twisted in her seat to face her grandfather. "Gramps, I'll never leave you..."—she turned back to Chad— "...or you again."

"Well then, a Valentine's Day toast to a new beginning."

"Valentine's Day? God, I've been so busy with everything...I forgot."

"We know, but we didn't forget. We wanted to surprise you, sweetie."

"Gramps, you two definitely did that."

As busboys and waiters flashed past them, they swirled the air around Victoria. Mikey's chest filled with her scent with each inhale, and each one deeper and longer than the last increased his desire for her. If he touched her right now, he didn't think he'd be able to stop. Hell, he was having just as hard a time not touching her. The glass of red wine in front of him was the closest thing to occupy his hand, so, he grabbed it, and took a long sip.

"The February 19th deadline is almost here. Do you need me or Gramps to do anything?" He wanted her to need him. To want him. For anything, the business, personal...especially personal. The more time he spent with her, the more he wanted to be with her in a way they hadn't been since high school, and then *it* drove her away. He knew he wouldn't be able to stand losing her again. This time, he would make sure she meant her words, and never left again.

"You guys have done so much. Now, we just need to finalize the photos, menu and prices, and that's it."

"Well, let's toast to possibilities."

"Possibilities."

"Possibilities."

Victoria paced back and forth in her bedroom knocking against footboards and dresser corners. The longer it took for the phone to be answered, the angrier she became. When he answered, she rambled irately. "Mikey, why did Rebecca call me congratulating me on being accepted as a vendor for both the Beale Street Music Festival and the

Sweet Victory

Barbeque competition?"

"Rebecca called you?"

"Yes." *Why didn't he answer the question?* "Why did she call me?"

"She's on the committee."

"You knew this, and didn't tell me."

"I didn't think it was important. You got your spot on your own. She was just one of four people."

"If that was the case, then why keep it a secret?"

"Because you probably wouldn't have done it, and I thought it was good for you to be a part of it. A way to make your own money, and not worry about finding a job you didn't like. So, that you wouldn't have a reason to leave."

"You want to make sure I stay, then you should've been honest with me. You should have told me you thought about it because of her." Deflated, she sank down onto her bed.

"Victoria, if I would've told you where I got the idea, you would've immediately rejected it. Even though it's a good idea. I'm right, and you know it."

"You know how I feel about Rebecca."

"Yeah, but we were kids and that was high school."

But, back then high school was her life, and it affected the rest of her life. Rebecca had a child with the man she loved. "Yeah. Stupid, I know, but..."

"Victoria, is there something we need to talk about?" The sound of his voice, made her want to jump through the phone, and say, "Yes. I'm still in love with you. Never stopped, and I'm extremely jealous of the fact that the two of you have a child."

Snap out of it. "Yes...no, it just surprised me when she called. You know how she can be." A *Bitch*!

"What did she say? Are you okay?"

"It's not important. I'm fine. We need to have things together before April 30th. They check your sales every night to ensure they get their 25%. They have a guarantee of a $2500 payment. And we need to get cash registers, tents, and product. There's a lot to do."

"Victoria, what's wrong?"

"Nothing."

"I can hear it in your voice."

"She's waiting for us...for me to fail."

"We won't fail."

"How do you know that? I have no idea what I'm doing. And I don't have money or help."

"You've got me."

"I know, and I couldn't do this without you. We got what we wanted, right? A spot in the Memphis in May festivities. But, I guess I'm scared. What if this doesn't work?" Before she could get her life together, she would have to face Rebecca. How do you face the woman that pushed you away from your home? The knot in her stomach twisted and kinked more.

"Trust me, Victory, this is a good thing. Together, we can make this work."

"Together?"

"Yes."

"But, what are we...what if our friendship ends?"

"Victory, I meant what I said at dinner on Valentine's Day. I don't plan on going anywhere. And I don't want you to go anywhere."

"I don't want to go anywhere, but if this doesn't work...if my money runs out, how will I take care of me and Gramps?"

81

Sweet Victory

"We'll figure this out together.   We'll talk about this more.   I just got a call over the radio."

"What if none of this works?"

"Then we'll do something else."

Chapter Eight

Victoria sucked in her breath as she grabbed the door, and pulled it open. A&R Barbeque was her last chance. She'd combed through every food vendor on the list for the Memphis in May Barbeque Competition for potential partners. Rebecca may have *allowed* her in, but she was going to make it successful. If she could find some vendors willing to carry her desserts, it would allow her to have additional selling points throughout the event, and maybe after the event, too. Phone call after phone call had produced mostly rejections. Except for three: Interstate, DeBones, and A&R. No one else would listen to her pitch. She'd already struck out twice. *Deep breath. God, help me.* Cinnamon. Hot sauce. Greens. A mixture of delightful smells rushed out of the door toward her.

She moved around the line of waiting patrons, and made her way to the counter. "Excuse me. I'm looking for Ms. Charmaine Harris. The restaurant manager."

"Ms. Charmaine," repeated the cashier.

"Yes, I have an appointment with her."

The young woman's warm smile was filled with curiosity. "Sure, have a seat over there, and I'll get her from the kitchen."

Moments later, Ms. Harris appeared, her apron soiled with everything Victoria smelled. She stood to greet her. "Hello Ms. Harris."

Sweet Victory

"Oh, please...call me Ms. Charmaine."

Victoria let the kindness in the woman's southern drawl wash over her, and erase her fear. "Ms. Charmaine."

"Now, how can I help you?"

"Well..."—Victoria sat her portfolio on the table, and opened her sample case. "...as we discussed on the phone, I wanted to speak with you about the possibility of adding my desserts to your booth at the barbeque cook off, and possibly here in the store, too."

Ms. Charmaine motioned toward the display cases near the registers. "Ms. Victoria, we have our own line of sweets."

"Yes, ma'am. I know, but you only carry peach cobbler, pecan pie, and a few cookies." She handed a copy of her menu to Ms. Charmaine. "I can provide you an assortment of cakes, cookies, and pies which will allow your cooks to focus on your delicious barbeque."

Ms. Charmaine glanced over her shoulder at the line of customers patiently waiting. "We could definitely use help with freeing up the staff a little especially right now while we gear up for the event."

Victoria handed Ms. Charmaine a small package of chocolate coconut candies. She watched as she unwrapped and tasted the sample. She didn't realize until Ms. Charmaine smiled that she'd been holding her breath.

"This is wonderful."

"Thank you. It's my grandmother's recipe."

"Perhaps we can set up an arrangement. Consignment."

"Consignment." Her heart sank a little. "Payment based on product movement only."

"Ms. Victoria, your product is delicious, and I can tell from what you've presented that you're a determined young lady, but until we have a history of sales we're gonna be testing customers' opinions."

Victoria knew she was right, and it was the best offer she'd received. She could possibly lose a lot of product, but if she started with the cookies and candies which had a longer shelf-life this might work. "Ms. Charmaine. I think that will work."

A huge smile that brightened Ms. Charmaine's eyes and warmed Victoria's heart spread across her face. "Great. We'll work out all of the particulars later. For now, I want you to sit, and enjoy a meal on me."

"Ms. Charmaine, you don't have to do that. I..."

"I won't hear of it." And with that, Ms. Charmaine disappeared into the kitchen, and the young cashier popped up in her place.

Sticky sweet moments later, Victory licked the barbeque sauce off her fingers as she dialed Mikey's number. "Can you come over tonight?"

Early evening, after she'd been forced to watch too many hours of WWE wrestling with Gramps and Mikey, Gramps took a taxi to visit some of his friends at the retirement home, and announced he would return late, very late, so they didn't have to worry about him.

After poking around on different websites for promotional products, Victory glanced up from her computer at a dozing Mikey. She was too wired because of A&R to sleep, so she decided to warm up her left-over barbeque. Sweet scents of cinnamon, and honey perfumed the air. As soon as the microwave dinged, she popped one of the rib tips into her mouth. Hot. She puffed out her cheeks, and sucked in air. After a moment, she sucked and chewed. "Mmm. Heavenly." She walked into the living room sucking barbeque sauce from her fingers.

"That looks good."

She stopped at the kitchen door. "Do you want some? I can put some on a plate for you, too."

"Come here."

The sound of his voice hinted at something, combined with smoky brown eyes, it sent a shiver through her that pooled between her legs.

She sat beside him.

"Victoria..."—he paused, but then he began again. "...I need to know if you feel what I feel."

"I..."

"No, listen for a sec. When you left, I understood. I didn't want to hold you back. I knew things here weren't good for you, and I know we had problems."

"Problems? I hurt you, and I thought...I thought you hated me. That you wouldn't be able to forgive me." She glanced at the food on the table. Suddenly, she'd lost her appetite.

"Forgive you?" He took one of her hands into his, and ran his fingers up and down her forearm. "I was angry for a long time. Really angry. I got into a lot of fights. Lost some friends. Made some enemies, but more than anything, I was pissed you'd made a decision like that by yourself. I thought we were friends more than anything."

"I'm sorry," she squeaked.

"No, I'm not saying this because I want an apology. I want you to know that I don't blame you for anything. We were kids, but we're not anymore."

"No, we're not." Some of the sadness on her heart

lifted.

"I want to be with you."

"God, I'm such a mess. What do I have to offer you?"

"What do you mean?"

"No job. Living off of my savings." She motioned toward the phone. "Bill collectors calling every hour."

"So, Valentine's Day dinner...our conversations since then?"

Labored breathing caught her words in her throat. "I meant what I said. I don't want to ever leave you. Or Gramps. But, nothing's changed. I'm still scared."

"Of what?"

"So many things: not being able to find a job, Gramps having to go to a worse home, or having to move again. But, also of disappointing you. Hurting you again. I don't know what I'm doing half the time."

"Victory, I'm agreeing to be a part of this, too."

"I don't think I could stand to lose you again." She knew she wouldn't be able to. Since the day he'd walked back into her life, she felt like it was right. But, if she took this step and messed up again...what would she do?

His voice lowered and softened. "You won't lose me."

He sat too close. His smell. His eyes. His touch confused her. She rose from the couch to place the container of food back in the fridge.

"Victory."

She kept walking. If she could get one moment without him so close, she could think.

"Victory, are you always going to walk away."

His words froze her to the two square feet where she

Sweet Victory

stood; he came to her.

He turned her to face him. The food in her hands blocked his advance. He set it on a nearby table. One by one, he licked the fingers that had been covered with barbeque sauce. With each touch of his tongue, a tingle traveled down her body.

"Mikey," she panted.

Kisses traveled from her fingers to the palm of her hand up her arm to her shoulder and neck.

"Mikey."

He kissed her cheek, her eyes, and finally, her lips. Memory didn't serve his kiss justice.

"Victoria, I don't want to stop. But, if you tell me to, I will."

Every ragged word begged her not to stop him.

"Mikey, I've missed your touch." No longer the touch of a young man, but the touch of a man who knew what he wanted. And at the moment, what he wanted was her.

"Baby, I've missed you." His hands slid up and down her torso. At her hips, they stopped. "I want you." The words were accented with a gentle push of his body against hers. "I want you." Another push.

Each touch of his body elicited a moan, and made the fire between her legs burn hotter.

His hand lifted her mouth to his. Passionately, his mouth took hers. Tangy sweet barbeque assaulted her senses. He tasted delicious.

Firm and confident, strong hands gripped her body and slid between her legs, then pressed them apart. His knee fit between them right above her knee. As his organ swelled, her excitement grew.

"I want to be with you, Victory."

"Don't stop."

The zipper of her pants slid open. The clothing that kept his body away from hers disappeared. The length of him slid against her. "I don't have anything. No protection."

"I'm on the pill." Her hands gripped and tugged at his bottom pulling him toward her.

"Baby." His response satisfied her.

"Mikey, I want to feel you."

With a firm tug, he pulled her into him again. Breathy words whispered. "You sure?"

She didn't want to run from him...ever again. She wanted to know him as a man. *Her* man. "Positive."

The tip of his penis teased. She wrapped a leg around his waist, and pressed her body into his. He concentrated: watching her reaction, and pleasuring himself as he guided his shaft into her welcoming body.

He filled and stretched her. The feel of him inside of her after so many years was similar to before, but different. No fumbling. No uncertainty. He knew exactly how to touch her body. The blouse she wore fell to the floor followed by her bra. His tongue tasted each nipple before settling on one breast. He pulled her bottom into him away from the wall causing her to arch her back and thrust her breasts forward. She used her hands to hold them, allowing him to alternate between them at his pleasure, and hers.

The grip of his hands around her waist made her feel wanted, needed. As his hands traveled the length of her body, she mumbled, "I remember the way you feel."

"Did you miss it?" he panted.

She bit the corner of her bottom lip, and leaned her head against the cool wall. "Yes." Stepping backwards, he gripped her, spun her around, and pulled her butt into his

Sweet Victory

groin angling her back.

"Good." The kiss on her shoulder traveled to her neck.

She didn't want to, but she pulled away, and spun around to face him. "I'm sorry." Tears began to roll down her cheeks. The hole she tried to fill had been crammed with a lot of things—a flashy car and an expensive townhouse, but never what she really wanted—him.

His fingers brushed at her tears. "When you left, I never thought I'd recover."

"I thought I had to leave to heal." As his fingers caressed her lips, she kissed them. One at a time. "I was wrong."

Sweat glistened on his chest. She couldn't resist running her fingers across it exploring his nipples, and the soft trail of blond hair leading to his still hard pulsating organ. She wrapped her hand around it, and slowly began to pump. His hands braced against the wall on either side of her. He leaned in, and ran his jaw against hers. "You were?"

"When I saw you on the highway, I knew I never should have left."

His head dipped, and he kissed her, slow, long, and deep. "Don't ever leave me again."

"It would take a natural disaster to take me away..."

His kiss covered her words. "Put me inside of you." His tongue toyed with her earlobe, and then traced a path down her neck.

She spread her legs, and teased. Staring into his brown eyes, she dared him. She lifted her body from the wall, and pressed her clit against the tip of his rod. Each push sent a tingle straight to her nipples. Her head leaned against the wall arching her breasts upward. He seized the moment, and suckled until she moaned.

"Put me inside, Victory. I want to feel you, again."

This time, she couldn't tease. The head of his penis slid inside her effortlessly. Her arms encircled his neck. For a moment, she pressed his mouth against her breast. "That feels good."

He lifted his head, and locked onto her eyes. One hand cupped her left breast, and massaged. The other slid around her butt, and pulled her tighter to him. His body felt as if it touched the back of her.

His mouth covered hers. She closed her eyes.

"Open your eyes."

With every touch of his hand, she lost her focus more. "Huh?"

He spoke against her lips. "I want you to know it's me."

How could she not know it was him? How could she ever confuse the way he felt inside of her? The touch of his body against hers made her come alive. Heat crawled over every inch of her skin, increasing in temperature where their two bodies connected. "I know it's you."

The thrusts of his body punctuated his words. "Don't ever leave me again." His hands gripped her hips to hold her in place.

Her body screamed at her, and a wonderful sensation shot through her causing her nipples to tingle. A thousand needles pricked her skin. Sweat rolled between her breasts. This time, she latched onto his nipple, and softly tugged with her teeth. The taste of salt blended with barbeque. Each scrape of her teeth and tease of her tongue received a response.

"I can't."

"I love you, Victory."

"I never stopped loving you."

91

Sweet Victory

His body jerked, once, twice, and then he released inside of her. Each burst throbbed, and etched itself into her memory; she never wanted to lose that feeling again.

Weeks of making up for twelve years of absence still hadn't tired them out. The only hindrance was Gramps. Two adults could only be so quiet. They'd ended in a fit of laughter the few times they'd tried to make love with Gramps in the house. Since their relationship had become sexual, she'd agreed to spend two nights a week at his apartment, but she didn't like leaving Gramps alone for too many nights. Mikey's bed was larger than hers, plenty of room for her to sprawl out, and she loved it, but as she ran her hands over the quilts she had to admit it was hard not to wonder why he needed such a big bed or who'd been in it before her, but that was her jealousy prodding her again.

Mikey hid his hands behind his back as he entered the bedroom. She settled back into the pillows as he nestled beside her. Except for his gun and shoes, he was fully dressed, and ready for work.

"I didn't know you had to go to work."

"Sorry baby, they called while you were sleep. A slot opened up at the last minute."

"I thought we'd have more of the evening together before I went home."

"Things will change when I take the Sergeants' test. But, for now, you know I need the extra money."

"I know. I'm not trying to be difficult."

"You're not." With a promising kiss, he changed the

subject.   "Baby, I know how you feel about some of the gang from high school, but think about attending the reunion." He dropped a yearbook and some papers on the bed.   Before she could pick them up, he'd nestled up to her in bed stroking her cheek with a look in his eye she had no defense against.   She couldn't stop kissing him, and didn't want him to stop either.   His hands slid underneath the covers following the curves of her body until it reached her thighs. The underwear he'd stripped from her the night before still lay on the chair across the room.   No defense as his fingers slid inside her.   The more he stroked her, the foggier her brain became.   She would say yes to anything he wanted, but not that freaking reunion.

"No."

He nibbled at her earlobe as his fingers became more determined.   "Come on, baby, I'll be there.   A lot of the guys would like to see you."   Slowly, his mouth traveled down her neck.   Each lick and bite he gave, she returned.   His fingers slid easily in and out of her body.   When his mouth latched onto her breast, she nearly exploded, but he pulled away. "Please baby, come with me."   The laughter in his voice implied he knew exactly what he was doing, and why he teased her.

The quickening of his rhythm between her legs, and the firmness of his grip on her nipple controlled her words, not her brain.   "Okay."   Soft laughter vibrated against her breast.   Her bottom rose from the bed in an effort to allow his fingers deeper access.   His thumb caressed her at the perfect moment, and her body climaxed.

Gently massaging her body with the palm of his hand, Mikey kissed her breast, then stood and walked to the closet. He returned with his gun and shoes.   The bulge in his pants showed she was not the only one affected by his actions, but he got what he wanted, and as her body settled, she fumed. "You cheated.   You cannot make me stick to that."

Sweet Victory

He laced up his work boots, and laughed. "Yeah, I can, and I will."

She folded her arms across her chest, and pouted like a three year old. "I am not going."

"You're not?" He stopped lacing his shoes. "Do I need to return to bed?" He glanced at his watch. "I've got a few minutes."

"It wouldn't work again. I am not going."

"We'll talk about this later tonight." He turned, and walked toward the front door.

She yelled behind him. "I'll be at home with Gramps when you get off."

The only response she received was laughter.

Chapter Nine

The hallways of her high school had not changed in twelve years. Glass cases filled with various trophies for basketball, baseball, and cheerleading lined the walls. Photos of homecoming queens, class presidents, and quarterbacks donned the walls. Conspicuously, her photo was absent from the cheer section. Mikey had convinced her to visit their high school before meeting the others at a nearby restaurant for dinner. Why? Each room they visited reminded her of too many things. The biology room she and Mikey used to sneak away to because it was always empty. The auditorium where they had study hall, but never studied. An ache formed behind her eyes. She closed them, and pinched the bridge of her nose.

"Hey..."—he placed a finger underneath her chin tipping her face so her eyes met his—"...is all of this making you sad?"

Beyond sad, really, but not because of what she saw because of what she'd missed. Twelve years of being with him. The chance to be the mother of his first child. She didn't even know what their baby was...boy or girl. "A little. I guess."

"That's not what I wanted. I wanted you to remember the way we used to love each other, and know how much I love you now."

It was funny how simple words could erase so much time and pain. "I love you, too. It's just that I lost so much here."

He dropped his hand from her chin, and pulled her body into his. His breath puffed against her hair as he spoke. "We were young." Slowly, his nose nuzzled her hair. With a quick brush of his hand, he swept her hair from her face, and lifted her lips to his. "I'd never let you get away that easily again."

She giggled softly against his lips. God, she didn't ever want him to let her go.

"Well, how quaint."

The snarky voice yanked her from her peace.

Mikey straightened, and pulled Victoria tight against his side. "Rebecca, what are you doing here?"

Rebecca's fair features mirrored her daughter's: blue eyes, keen nose, and narrow chin. On Paige, combined with the beautiful blond locks of her father, it was beautiful. With Rebecca, it mocked a Dickens' cartoon character. With her entourage behind her, Victoria expected them to break out in Christmas carols at any minute.

"What? We can't visit our school?" She looked back at her group. "So, Victoria, how have you been? And like I told Chad, I can't wait to taste your stuff at Memphis in May. You know you almost didn't make it. It was hard convincing the committee to let you in. We have so many local cooks that have great desserts. And they've all been to culinary school."

Victoria took a step forward, but Mikey's grip on her waist held her in place. "Rebecca," she ground out. "It's been a long time. I guess I should thank you *if* you convinced the committee in my favor." Knowing Rebecca the way she did, she was certain any debate over her involving Rebecca was not in her favor.

An angled smile lit Rebecca's face. "I felt in my heart..."—her hand rose to her heart—"...that it was the right thing to do. You know...helping an old friend."

"Helping an old friend?"

Tiffany's, one of Rebecca's minions, blonde curls bounced around her face as her head bobbed with her words. "Oh sure, we heard that you lost your job and everything."

"Tiffany, I didn't lose my job. I quit. Tell me, where'd you get your information?" Tiffany didn't answer, but her head swiveled toward Rebecca.

"Chad told me when he picked up the information from my house late one night," she smiled.

Rebecca's words stung, but she wasn't seventeen any longer, and she knew somewhere in those words was a lie. She'd talk about that with Mikey in private.

"Rebecca, stop your lying. I never told you anything about Victoria."

Standing in the halls of their high school surrounded by so many memories: bad and good, Mikey's defense of her against more lies from Rebecca somehow made everything in their past fade further away.

"I don't know how you found out anything about anything, but we really don't have time for it tonight." Mikey's hand slid from her waist to grab her hand. "We've got to go."

"We'll see you at the reunion dinner." The words lagged in the hallway behind them.

Coincidence or not, everyone had agreed to have dinner at The Cadre. The Cadre was where Mikey and Rebecca were to have been wed. If Mikey hadn't found out Rebecca lied about being pregnant, this would have been the scene of the crime. Personally, Victoria would have chosen The Chapel:

much more quaint, but that was her. As old as The Peabody, The Cadre sat in Midtown where lots of old Memphis money lived. The Cadre was the perfect location for Rebecca and her social climbing parents to lavishly display their connections to money. Rebecca must have spit bullets when Mikey became a police officer instead of a lawyer like his father. Rebecca's law degree from the University of Memphis hadn't landed her the husband or lifestyle she'd dreamed of. So, maybe, the father of her child being a blue collar union man was better than no man. But, this time, Victoria wouldn't run away, and give him up. She couldn't hold back the snicker that escaped as she sipped her water.

"Hey, you okay?" Mikey's hand rubbed in small circles on her back. The heat his touch generated spread much further.

A quick glance at him, and possession grabbed her. "Oh, yeah, I'm fine, just thinking." She leaned over, and softly kissed him on the cheek. She knew a small smile curved her lips.

Mikey stared without a word for a moment. "Hmm, okay."

She watched his eyes narrow and focus on her mouth as she playfully bit at the corner of her lip. Everyone began firing questions.

"How's your grandfather?" asked Tiffany

"Fine, thanks for asking," she responded.

"How'd you and Chad reconnect?" Rebecca spat out.

Staring into her eyes, not at Rebecca, Mikey answered, "I rescued her."

"From what this time?"

"Rebecca, what the fu..." Mikey's words were cut off.

"So, tell us, Victoria, why'd you come back home?" asked Jason, one of Chad's varsity basketball teammates. Jason still looked the same. His muscled arms hadn't lost any of their girth over the years. A Marine issued buzz cut coupled with shadowy grey eyes had trapped a lot of girls behind bleachers in the gym. Two of them: Tiffany and Rebecca, were at the table.

No one spoke, ate, or drank. They sat almost without motion waiting on her response. She didn't know if it was a set-up question or not. Jason had always been a pretty decent guy, even if his taste in women was not.

"Hey, Jason, I told you Victoria's back to be with her grandfather."

Victoria hadn't realized she'd frozen until she heard Mikey's words, and felt his hand rest on hers underneath the table.

"Yeah, I came back to be with Gramps, and now I have the business." Why not be honest with everyone, including herself? "But, like so many other people, my company cutback a lot of employees..."

Laughter interrupted her speech. She glared in the direction it came from.

"...so, to save my employees' jobs, I quit."

The laughter quieted, and everyone sat, waiting.

"Well, damn, Victory you'll never change. Always doing something for somebody," said Jason.

The slap of a glass against the table drew everyone's attention. "Whatever."

"Rebecca, what is your problem?" she asked.

"You."

Well, that was pretty straight forward. "What about me?"

"You come back here like we're supposed to be so happy to see you or something."

Sweet Victory

The high ceilings, and large rooms of The Cadre amplified their voices. Other patrons' heads turned in their direction. Victoria had no desire to create a scene. She softened her voice. "Happy to see me?" Again, all eyes were on her. "No one has to be happy to see me..."—she shifted in her chair to face Mikey—"...but, I am happy to see you."

He leaned in and whispered, "Tonight is going to be a lot of fun." The touch of his lips against her cheek sent tingles down her arms. She couldn't wait to get him home. And his words and actions, gave her courage to continue.

With Mikey's hand in hers, she turned to face Rebecca again. "Rebecca, I don't need anything from you. I'm here because I wanted to see old friends. Now, if you have a problem with me, well, then you shouldn't have come."

Rebecca's voice rose and octave or two. "The problem is you! It's you who's jealous of my child with Chad." With each word, you could see the mouthful of food she hadn't chewed.

"What the hell do you mean she..." With a soft tap of their joined hands to his thigh, Victoria, cut off Mikey's statement.

Anger rolled in waves over her entire body. If she could start fires with her mind, The Cadre, and all of its historic decoration would go up like cheap plywood.

"No," she searched her heart. "I'm not jealous." *Not anymore.* "But, I do think you are fortunate to have a child with a man like Mikey. He provides for his daughter, loves her, and doesn't think about himself. All women want a child with a man like that."

The other women at the table heads nodded in silent support, and the men smiled in agreement.

"What? Care for his daughter? What does he tell you? I take care of my child." Rebecca flicked her napkin at Chad. "He's nothing but a freaking cop. He doesn't have anything.

No money."

Victoria's grip on Mikey's hand tightened.   She didn't have to look at him to know he would have that intense basketball face on.   The one he used whenever he concentrated to keep outside noise to a minimum during a game.   In her mind, she saw his tight mouth, his features blank, and mirrored them.

"Rebecca, what the fuck do you mean? I don't take care of my child?"   She tried to calm him down, but he continued. "Why in the hell am I killing myself with overtime and part-time work?   Because I have to pay Paige's tuition..."

"Private school is expensive.   What?   Do you want my daughter to be in a 'regular' school?"

"Only because I can't change it, she's there for now. Tuition and child support are kicking my ass.   You think it will make a difference with my family or me.   That I'll change my mind, and marry you?"

"What...I don't want you to marry me."

Victory couldn't resist jumping in.   "If that's the case, then why are you still acting like you're in high school?   We came here to have dinner with old friends.   But, you're busy trying to show everybody how you're so much better than me. *Why?*"   She pointed at Mikey.   "Isn't it all about *him*?   The man you *claim* you don't want.   Or, is it just that he doesn't want you?"

Silence stilled the table.

Rebecca glared at Victoria from the other end of the table.   She opened her mouth preparing to say something, then suddenly grabbed her throat.   Like a mindless severed appendage, her hand reached out for her water glass.   Her natural healthy pink complexion morphed into a deep hot pink.   The water glass toppled to the table; spilling on the freshly pressed white linen.

Sweet Victory

Tiffany jumped up from her chair. "Oh my God, I think she's choking."

Jason circled the table, grabbed Rebecca, encircled her in his arms, and squeezed. A piece of fish popped out, and landed in her salad.

Tiffany handed Rebecca the glass of water in front of her as everyone else stared at each other. Amazed at all that had occurred, no one said anything.

"Listen, we're going to settle our part of the bill, and leave, but Jason, and everyone we'll see you at the reunion." Mikey called a waiter, and paid. "Hell of a dinner."

Chapter Ten

Weeks after that horrible dinner of nightmares, Victoria ripped herself out of bed, and away from Mikey. She would have given anything to spend the whole day lying beside him, but she had to make it to the packager. He wanted to go with her, but he needed the overtime. She understood. Nothing was immediate, but she had sunk a huge chunk of her retirement into Sweet Victory, and if it didn't pay off, she didn't know what she'd do. So, she couldn't stop him from doing what he needed. Paige's tuition was expensive, and he was saving for a bigger place. He needed the overtime.

The packager/distributor Victoria had settled on was perfect. Their facility was huge, and there would be no problem preparing what product she needed for The Beale Street Music Festival, the first leg of Memphis in May. They had plenty of refrigerators, stoves, and the size of the space itself amazed her. If she had ten people in the room there'd still be space for ten more. She couldn't wait to tell Mikey all about it. A special meal to commemorate the whole thing, and she'd show Mikey and Gramps everything.

"Hey, Victory darling, what you doing in here?"

Whoosh. Juice spilled across the kitchen floor. She knelt, and mopped the spill up with a dish rag. Victoria's excitement had her buzzing around the kitchen so fast, she hadn't noticed when her grandfather walked in. "Nothing, Gramps. Just making dinner. Did I wake you from your nap?"

"It's okay. It smells delicious in here." He made his way over to the pots on the stove. Lifting lids, he sniffed his way from back to front.

"Careful, Gramps, that stuff is really hot."

"Mmm, black-eyed peas, turnip greens, and smoked turkey."

She watched as her grandfather's eyes glazed over, and he patted his stomach.

"Gramps, we've got to wait for Mikey."

"What time will he be home?"

"I'm not sure." She rinsed her hands, and grabbed the cordless phone on the counter. "Let me call him."

He picked up on the first ring. "Hello."

"Hey, what time will you be here?"

"Sorry, baby, but I've got a chance to work a few more hours. And I don't want to wake Gramps. So, I'll crash at the apartment tonight."

Acting like a child wouldn't make things better. "Okay."

"I promise I'll make it up to you. I want to hear about the packager."

"Tell Mikey to hurry. I'm hungry."

She threw her hand over the receiver, but she was sure Mikey heard anyway. She didn't want him to feel guilty for not showing up.

"What's Gramps talking about?"

"Oh, nothing. Don't worry about it. Just call me tomorrow."

"Victoria..."

"It's okay, really. I can do something else tomorrow."

"Forgive me."

The only thing she'd wanted all day was to see him, curl up beside him, and hold on. "Of course."

"I'll be there when you wake up."

"Promise?" If she couldn't have him that night, she'd definitely take him first thing in the morning.

"Promise."

"Good night. I love you."

"I love you, too. Good night."

His words ghosted through her mind exciting her more each time she thought of them.

"Well, Gramps, grab a seat. It's you and me tonight."

"I don't think it'll be that way for long." Gramps busied himself with pulling up a chair, and made a fuss over the food she placed in front of him. He sniffed the whole plate before grabbing his fork.

"Huh, what are you talking about, Gramps?"

After a silent grace, he opened his eyes, and said, "Mikey will be here after work, right?"

"Yeah."

"We don't have a lot of time for the two of us. I like having you to myself."

"I missed you, Gramps, and...I'm sorry it took me so long to come back home."

His hand covered hers. She covered it with her other hand. It felt so frail; he was so thin except for his little belly. So many years, birthdays, had not been celebrated. How many more would she be blessed to share with him.

"I love you, sweetie. It's okay. You're home, now."

Sweet Victory

"No, it's not, Gramps.   I ran away from home...from you."

"At eighteen you left home for college."

"Gramps, when she..."—suddenly, she couldn't look him in the eyes any longer.   "...died, I was lost."

"I know."

"Dad was crazy and abusive, and in jail.   Mom was gone.   Grandma protected me."

"I know."

She mustered up the courage to face the look of anger she knew must be in his eyes.   "Gramps, I forgot that two people protected and cared for me, not just one."   His eyes showed no anger.   Instead, she thought maybe relief or joy. "Gramps, I love you, and I should have come back home a long time ago."

"No, baby, you needed to take time to let your heart heal.   To figure out what you needed."   He lifted her hands to his cheek, and then kissed them.   "I've missed you, and I'm glad to have our family together again."

"Gramps, how can you forgive me so easily?"

"I love you.   And baby don't you know, that's what family and love is about, forgiveness."

True to his word, the next morning Mikey was there, but he was not alone.   Half awake, she slept walked toward the smell of coffee and bacon.   Laughter greeted her at the door.   Mikey and Gramps, but there was a laugh she didn't recognize.   Soft and light, it floated above the two men.

Mikey stood as she entered, and kissed her on the cheek. "Hey baby, we..."—he nodded at the people at the table—"...didn't think you'd ever wake up."

So petite, she was nearly covered by the table. But, those curls would have given her away on any day. *Paige.* She tugged at her robe, suddenly embarrassed by the short silky fabric. "What time is it?" She turned to go back to her room. "Let me change. I'll be right back."

Mikey reached for her arm, and stopped her. "Babe, sit." He glanced across the table. "Paige, this is the friend I wanted you to meet."

"Hi, Miss Victoria."

Miss Victoria! "Hi, sweetie."

"Daddy said that we're going to go bowling today."

"Bowling?"

"Yeah, I thought we could all spend the day together."

"Babe, I have so much to do for Memphis in May, and we have the reunion coming up, too. I want to get something to wear for that." She sat, and Mikey placed a heaping plate of pancakes and sausage in front of her. Next came a huge scoop of gravy. If she ate what was on her plate, she'd gain fifty pounds. She would definitely have to keep Gramps and Mikey out of the kitchen.

"Victory, I think you young people should get out, and have a little fun."

"Gramps, what about you? What do you have planned or do you want to come with us."

"Ya'll don't need an old man like me hanging around."

"Sir, we'd love for you to join us. Right Paige?"

"Yes, sir. It's gonna be a lot of fun." The little blonde beauty beamed at everyone in the room.

107

Sweet Victory

Gramps popped the last of his pancakes into his mouth. "Well then, let's get ourselves together, and get out of here."

What felt like moments, but had actually been hours of banging bowling pins and happy squeals had left pizza crust, stale nachos, and half-eaten potato skins littering the table in front of Victoria.   Once again Paige ran down the lane attempting to roll her ball to knock down the pins.   If not for the bumper pads, her ball would have ended up in the gutters.   But, the little girl giggled in delight as the ball crawled slowly down the lane managing to knock down one pin before dropping into the gutter.

Paige turned and ran toward Victoria.   "Did you see me hit the pin, Miss Victoria?"   Every curl on Paige's head flew in a different direction as she jumped up and down in the air.

Victoria couldn't resist...she scooped the little girl up, and hugged her.   "Yes.   Good job."   Paige's small arms circled her neck.   Victoria didn't expect it, but sadness and joy flowed through her at the same time.   The pain, guilt and loss, she'd managed to push down for so many years reared its head again.   The more it ached and pained her, the tighter she held Paige.

"What are we celebrating?" asked Mikey.

"We're celebrating Paige.   She knocked down a pin."

He handed the sodas he carried to Gramps, and swooped Paige from Victoria's arms.   "Wow, sweetie.   We might have to let you go pro."

Angelic giggles wafted through the air above rocking falling pins, people yelling and cursing, and music playing. Every time she heard a curse word, she searched the crowd for the culprit.   If she found them, she'd ask them if they noticed the beautiful little child beside her hearing every word.

Grunts to her right drew her attention. "Hey Gramps, are you okay?"

"I'm fine. I could use a little nap, but I can't remember when I've had so much fun."

Her non-medical review of her grandfather didn't sit well with her. "Hey Gramps, I don't like your color. You're awfully pale." She picked up a glass of water from the table. "Here drink this."

He swatted at her hand. "Stop worrying about me. We're here to have fun." She watched as he twisted in his seat. "Is your back okay?"

"I'm fine young lady."

"Hmm. Gramps, I'm going to make you a doctor's appointment first thing in the morning."

"Sweetie, let's just enjoy today," he relaxed into the padded bench, and watched the action around him with a smile. "Today, we're a family again. I waited so long for this."

Chapter Eleven

The weeks between strolling through the halls of her high school with Mikey, and the reunion blurred. As she scanned the room, she decided the reunion committee should be shot. What made anyone think the styles of the 90s were cool? God, if she saw one more thirty year-old woman walk past her with big hair, too much make-up, and baggy clothes, she would scream.

The other guests of the Marriott did double-takes at each member of her graduating class as they came and went from their ballroom. Some of the younger guests, who weren't even born in '92 didn't hide their laughter at all.

Instead of going with the gaudy prom dress idea, she decided to wear her cheerleader outfit. Why not? Everyone had their opinions about her, and why she left. They'd kicked her off the cheer squad, ridiculed and ostracized, but she still had had a successful career, and now, she was back.

Mikey wore the old jersey she wore the night he rescued her, a tad faded, but he didn't care. The chest of the boy, and the body of the man did different things to that shirt. His chest stretched each faded letter of the logo...V-A-R-S-I, the rest of the letters had washed away. At the sign-in table, she paused, and tugged at her skirt.

Mikey's hand left hers, and his arm wrapped around her waist. A brush of Mikey's lips against hers faded everything around her to black. "You ready for this?"

Sweet Victory

"As much as I guess I'll ever be."

Jennifer, another one of her ex-cheer squad members, shot her a wide-eyed glare that said tons. She and Mikey took their name tags, and entered the ballroom with whispers and giggles at their backs. Orange and blue streamers, balloons, and decorations adorned the room clashing with the crystal chandeliers, and wood molding.

"God, who was on the decorating committee?"

"I will give you one guess," answered Mikey.

Mrs. White, her former cheer coach, caught her first. "Hi, Victoria."

Mikey's grip around her waist tightened. "Hi, Mrs. White. How have you been?"

"Well. Thank you." Her pudgy index finger circled the rim of the small glass of orange punch she held. "I hope you've been well, too?" The words were punctuated with tightly drawn eyebrows.

"Yes, I have. Thank you so much."

A timid smile crossed her pale face. "Good. Good." A little of the tiredness in her eyes disappeared. Mrs. White took a few steps back, and observed Victoria. And Victoria did the same. A few pounds heavier, with a head full of grey hair, but Mrs. White looked the same. "That uniform still looks great on you. I bet you still have all the moves."

"I don't know. I haven't done anything since high school."

The small light in her eyes dimmed. "Victoria, we all owe you an apology. By the time we knew the truth, you were gone. We tried to contact you." She glanced at Mikey. "Chad even went to D.C. to talk to you, but nothing worked."

What? When did he do that? Her head whipped toward Mikey, then back to Mrs. White. "After I started college, I just wanted to put everything behind me."

"I understand, and it looks like you did a great job at that. I heard you have begun your own business, and that you'll be participating in Memphis in May."

"Really? How did you know?"

"Memphis is only so big, plus my cousin is on the committee. She told me she had a submission from a cheerleader from my school that just returned to the area. I knew it was you before she said your name."

"Did you help me?"

"I didn't really have to. She said your partnership with A&R Barbeque was one of the key factors in your favor. And almost everyone on the committee agreed."

So, that's one of the reasons Rebecca had to fight with the committee. She glanced at Mikey, and they both laughed. Mrs. White stared at them both curiously.

"What's funny?"

"Oh, nothing, I knew Rebecca was on the committee, but she told me it was hard to get people to decide to let me sell."

Mrs. White's wrinkled brow smoothed with understanding, and all three of them began to laugh. Other faculty, and friends joined them, and the music swelled. Someone yelled, "Let's get this party started." Time filled with hugs, kisses, stares, and orange punch. She actually enjoyed herself.

"Excuse us. Excuse us."

The crowd parted.

Both, she and Mikey turned toward the voice. Mikey's hand released her waist, as he dropped to his knees, and threw his arms wide open in welcome. "Hey, baby." Tiny Paige Kirkpatrick clad in her mother's cheer uniform, pulled her smiling mother through the crowd.

Sweet Victory

Paige let go of her mom, and ran to her dad. She flung herself into his arms. "Hey, Daddy. I've missed you."

"I've missed you, too. What are you doing here?"

She looked over her shoulder at Rebecca. "Mom said I could be her date tonight."

Mikey glanced over Paige at her mother. "Did she?" He tugged at her skirt. "And what are you wearing?"

"It's Mom's. She had it done to fit me." Paige slid from her father's arms, and did a little twirl on the floor.

"Hey, Miss Victoria, we look alike."

"Yes, we do. We'd be the best team ever."

"Yeah, just like when we went bowling."

Mikey stalked toward Rebecca, but stopped just short of her. "Why would you bring her here?"

"She's *my* daughter. I can take here wherever I choose."

He looked around the room. "And you think this is an appropriate place. Drinking. Dancing. Adults being adults."

"I don't need permission from *you* for anything."

"True. But, don't you think about how all of this affects *our* daughter. Damn, you will never change. Always playing some stupid game."

"I'm not playing games." She took a step back. "You haven't said anything about my outfit."

He turned and reached for Paige. "Come on sweetie, let me take my two favorite cheerleaders for some punch."

Again, the crowd parted, and they left Rebecca standing with big hair, and a micro-mini.

After waiting for them on the side of the dance floor while another song played, Rebecca clicked her way across the room in her hooker boots, and grabbed Paige's hand. "Don't you want to dance with your mom, too?"

"Sure, Mom. I just liked being a cheerleader with Miss Victoria."

"Can you go and get me a glass of punch?" She pointed at Tiffany standing on the side of the dance floor. "Aunt Tiffany wanted you to dance with her, too."

"Okay. I'll be right back, Dad." The crowd swallowed Paige's tiny frame, and blonde curls.

Rebecca turned toward them, and unleashed. "How much do you have *her*..."—she flung a finger in Victoria's direction—"...around *my* daughter?"

Victoria wanted to scratch at her eyes...*her*...*my* daughter. Mikey's body stiffened. One arm reached out, and snaked around Victoria, pushing her behind him. "What do you mean *her* around *your* daughter? She's my daughter, too."

"I don't think it's healthy for you to have all of your women around Paige. She's impressionable at this age, and we wouldn't want her to pick up any bad habits."

"All of my women? Bad habits? She would learn *those* from you...wouldn't she?"

Victoria tapped Mikey on the shoulder. "Paige is coming back with punch."

He scanned the room, and signaled Jason. He pointed at Paige, and Jason stepped in. At first, she protested, but then, she sipped from the punch, and they went back toward Tiffany.

"Hey, we can do this somewhere else," interjected Victoria.

"Someplace else, why? You don't want people to see you with my leftovers," spat Rebecca.

Sweet Victory

"Leftovers?" Victoria stepped in front of Mikey. "I don't see it that way."

"Please. I'm a lawyer; people would kill to drive my Range Rover, and I don't need Chad's child support to help pay for my house in Germantown or Paige's school. I do it all myself. Why would I need him?"

"That's a lie Rebecca, and you know it. And what about Paige?" asked Mikey from beside Victoria.

"What about her?"

"You're rattling off your list of successes, isn't she on that list?"

Rebecca's face flushed red. "She's the best thing that ever happened to me, even if you are her father." One of her boot-clad feet stamped against the hardwood dance floor. "I don't know why I wasted so much time with you in high school or after. I should have known you wouldn't be like your father." She stalked forward, and jabbed a finger into his chest. "You always spent all of your time with her..."—she paused, and stared at Victoria—"...and why? She didn't want you or anything you gave her." A vicious sneer crossed Rebecca's face. The crowd closed in around them. Mrs. White and a few of the other teachers and coaches pushed through the crowd. The sneer on Rebecca's face widened.

"Rebecca, stop it," said Mikey as he pushed her hand away.

"No, it's okay, Mikey. Let her say what's on her mind. I don't care. She can't hurt me."

"No, I guess I can't hurt you." She nodded toward Mikey. "Not like you hurt him."

"Rebecca, this is a reunion, not a high school grudge match." Mrs. White spoke with a tone of authority from the front of the crowd.

Someone instructed the DJ to begin playing music

116

again, which at some point had stopped, but Victoria couldn't remember when that'd happened.

"What's your point, Rebecca?"

"My point is that I gave Chad the thing he wanted most. A child. Especially after you took one from him." The smile Rebecca had been holding back bloomed.

"What?" Victoria's body tensed. How did Rebecca know about that? Only her grandparents and Mikey knew. Memphis wasn't big, but the clinic she'd gone to had privacy rules. All of the anger flowing through her body targeted Rebecca. "How do you know about that?"

Rebecca's body relaxed. She straightened her back, and brushed at invisible dust on her skirt. After fiddling with her hair, she answered. "How do you think I know?" Both women and the audience around them focused on Chad. "Your precious little Mikey told me."

Jason and other members of the basketball team flanked Mikey and Victoria. Jason took a step forward which made Rebecca take a few steps back.

"Shut the hell up, Rebecca?" Mikey's blank expression told nothing. "Now." A slight lean forward of his body warned of unknown actions, and increased the intensity. Victoria watched as the muscles in his jaw tensed, and his breathing grew more and more shallow. With each breath, his mask of calm cracked. Suddenly his attention turned from Rebecca to her. He turned toward Victoria, and softened his tone. "Baby, let me explain..."

"There's nothing to explain, Mikey." Rebecca mimicked Victoria's voice. "If it wasn't for you, I wouldn't know she aborted your child, right?" Victoria didn't think it was possible for the crowd to become quieter, but they did. They didn't miss a word Rebecca said. "When you left and moved to D.C., he and I spent a lot of time together. We'd hang out. Go drinking." She ran her hands up and down her outfit, and winked at Mikey. "This was one of your favorites on me..."

"Rebecca, stop." This time, the warning came from Jason. The rest of the team began to disperse the attentive crowd. "Why are you acting like you're still in high school?"

"I'm not, she is..."—she pointed at Victoria—"...wearing her high school cheerleading outfit..."—she rolled her eyes—"...how pathetic."

"Pathetic, huh? Like showing up here with your child to try to purposely humiliate me? And for what? To get a man that you say you don't want, and you claim isn't good enough for you." Victoria stood for a moment, and glanced back and forth between Mikey and Rebecca. The crowd around her had thinned, but still everyone knew her secret, and even in their distant corners they waited to see what would happen next. The crazy voice inside her head wanted to give them what they waited for—a knock down roll around on the ground cat fight. In that skirt and heels, Rebecca wouldn't be able to do much of anything. She could wrap her hands in her shiny hair and yank her right down to the ground. "You know, I'm tired of all of this. I'm tired of you. My life is not for your entertainment. Fuck you!" Victoria didn't come to the reunion to make a scene, but she had let Rebecca under her skin. Why? She turned to Mikey. "How could you tell her something so private?" Tears welled up in her eyes. "I never...I never meant to..."—Mikey grabbed her arm, and pulled her away from Rebecca and the prying eyes of their audience. "I never meant to hurt you Mikey. I didn't think I could be a mother. I didn't know how to be."

His fingers brushed tears from her cheeks, and his lips touched the spot where they'd landed. Shielding her from the crowd behind them, he pressed her against a wall, and stood in front of her. The tears fell harder. "Who was going to teach me how to be a mother? I didn't have one."

"You had Gramps and your grandmother."

"Yeah, but what did I know about being a parent? We were teenagers. What if I would have been like her? Making bad choices?"

"You made better choices in men." He kissed her forehead. "I would never intentionally hurt you."

Her fingers slipped through his curls. God, she loved the way it felt to touch him. "I did, but I left that wonderful man, and ran away. What kind of mother screws up constantly, huh?" Her eyes fell to the ground. She couldn't dare to look into his eyes. "Can I apologize enough? Can I make things better? I just...I don't know."

"Why do you doubt so much? Just give us a chance. I know you're scared, but you've got to stop running away."

"I'm not..."

"Yes, you are."

"Do you really believe I would tell her anything about us, our loss?"

"I don't know..."

"When will you start believing in me? In the love I have for you?" This time, he turned and walked away. The crowd swallowed him.

God, no. Victoria ran through the crowd out of the ballroom into the parking lot. There he was. Stomping his way toward the car. "Mikey. Stop. Please."

Her plea went unanswered.

Tears flowed down her cheeks as she ran. If he made it

to his car before she caught up to him, she felt as if her heart would explode. He would leave her, and she'd never get him back. He wouldn't keep forgiving her...no matter what Gramps says. At the car, he stopped and turned to her. "Mikey, please listen to me. Please forgive me."

He opened her car door for her, and waited. At the door, she stared up into his eyes. The pain of her words, of her doubt, had dulled beautiful blue eyes filling them with sadness. She wished she could kiss away the pain her words had caused.

She kissed him, and he let her linger inhaling his scent before he stepped away. The salt of her tears covered his lips.

"I need to explain some things about what Rebecca said, but not here. Get in."

Chapter Twelve

Bubbles floated into the air from their bath. Victoria kicked at them with her foot, and then rested her leg back into the warm water surrounding them. Mikey fed her a piece of chocolate, and a sip of wine. The cold wine slipped down her throat warming her body more. Mikey's wet warm skin at her back supported her as she slid further under the blanket of bubbles.

"I'm sorry about what Rebecca said. It's not like it seemed."

"But, it was true."

"Yeah, but I didn't tell her."

Soapy water sloshed as Victoria turned to face Mikey. "Don't lie."

"I'm not." He sipped from his wine, and began again. "I didn't tell her, she found some of the letters I'd written you that you returned."

"The letters, but..."

"Yeah, after I caught her snooping, I stored them at Gramps' instead of throwing them away. I don't know why. I should have trashed them, but I guess I couldn't."

"And when did you move to my grandparents' house?"

"I lived there for a while right after high school because

Sweet Victory

I didn't know what I wanted to do. After I found out she wasn't pregnant, I wrote you. You didn't answer, so I drove up."

"When I was in college?" Parties and internships filled Victoria's days then.

"I got to the dorm Gramps said you lived in on a Saturday night. I thought I would find you sad...missing me," he laughed. "But, it didn't seem like you missed me at all. I saw you leave your dorm with some guy. I guess you were going on a date." His eyes roamed the curves of her bare bosom to the point where they dipped into the water. Victoria pushed her hands through the water breaking his stare. A slow smile curved his lips, and a hand dipped beneath the water. "Did you miss me?"

The wine in his glass disappeared, and he set the glass on the floor beside the tub. One hand rested on the side of the tub, and the other slipped back beneath the bubbles.

"Of course, but..." The water around him rippled back and forth, and the bubbles started to spread. "...I hurt you, and myself. I wanted to forget. I dated a lot."

"The guy you were with that night was tall, 6'4" or 6'5". Dark-skinned black guy."

"You remember him that well?"

"You don't?"

"I dated a lot. I had just walked away from you, my family, and aborted my child. I never let anybody hang around long." Wet fingers trailed across his jawline. "But, you know I loved jocks. I think he played for the basketball team. I guess I couldn't totally forget you." She smiled.

"So, what happened with him?"

Come on, Mikey, do you expect me to remember?"

The water around him stopped moving. "I don't believe you."

"That was years ago."

"I guess so, but don't do that to me again."

"Do what?"

"Try to erase me from your life."

"I wasn't..."

"Yes, you were."

"I just..."

"I know..."—his head leaned against the wall behind him—"... I guess I tried to do the same thing with Rebecca back then, and when you first came back home I tried to keep away." He leaned forward, and wrapped an arm around her, sliding her backward into his body. His hard erect body pressed against her bottom. "I think that's why Rebecca has such a hard time with you, with us. She saw those letters, knew who I wanted, and what we'd lost, and before I knew it...she was pregnant."

"Did you try to have a baby?"

"I always used a condom, and she told me she was on the pill, but it didn't seem to matter. And you were in D.C. You didn't seem to want anything to do with me. I was kind of lost."

"That not true. I loved you. I didn't know how to face you after what I'd done. I was lost, too." She could barely face herself. It wasn't just about aborting their baby...she was young, and they were stupid. They should have used protection. It was about not telling him before she did it. She wanted her cheerleading scholarships, and to go to college before she had a child. Even more she was afraid she'd be the same type of woman her mother was. A woman that had so many issues it ripped her away from her family, permanently, and left her elderly parents to raise a grandchild.

His grip around her waist tightened, and his hands

Sweet Victory

wandered up and down her body beneath the water. "The moment Paige was born I fell in love with her, but I only had half of what I wanted." His hands caressed her thighs. "I guess I was okay with the simple life here at home...wife and kids, with you, would have been perfect for me, but I know you wanted more than that."

"I wasn't ready, but it was no excuse for not talking with you about everything."

"You're here now." A warm wet hand stroked her cheek. "Are you ready, now?"

"The only thing I know is that I love you, and I want to be with you."

"I'll accept that answer, today."

Her head fell back onto his chest, and his hands slid between her legs slowly spreading them apart. The touch of his hands against her thighs upped the temperature of the water around them. The feel of his excitement against her back, and the intensity of her own need made her grind her body against his. Slow, deep circles pushed her butt against him. Each push yielded a moan. His hands slid up her stomach toward her breasts. Anticipation of his touch tightened her nipples. Both of his hands massaged her breasts. "Umm." Her hand dipped between her legs. Underneath the water, she could still feel the slickness of her body.

Mikey's tongue slid over her neck to her ear. Gently, he played with her earlobe before focusing on her mouth. With her head resting against his chest she gave in to her desires. The kiss released every pinned up emotion inside of her. He knew everything about her: fears about her mother, pain over the loss of her grandmother and abandonment of her grandfather, regrets about their child, and her dislike of Rebecca. The deeper he searched her mouth, the deeper and harder her fingers explored her own body. A soft squeeze of her nipples almost sent her over the edge.

He spoke into her wet hair. "If I keep watching you do that, I'm going to really lose it."

She pulled her hands away. "So, I should stop?"

He grabbed her hands. "No, but I'd like to join in."

Guiding his fingers into her body, Victoria's body melted against his. As she stretched her arms behind her mandarin scented water rolled down her body, she wrapped them around his neck, and gave her body to his hands.

His breath tickled her ear as he spoke. "I'll make sure you can't forget me again."

"Right here with you is where I want to be forever."

Chapter Thirteen

Victoria showed up at the packager's warehouses at 3:00 P.M. exactly. The doors were locked, and no one appeared to be inside. A few other cars littered the lot, but unlike the first few times she'd visited, there was no hustle and bustle. This part of Memphis was strictly industrial, nothing but factories: most abandoned, but some still operated offering a few jobs to hardworking people in the surrounding communities. Factories that used to thrive producing: fans, auto parts, meat packing, and more sat forgotten. Wasted. Even an empty army depot stood on several acres of wasted land nearby.

She pulled out her cell phone, and dialed Tony Daniels, her contact.

"Hello."

"Hello, Tony. This is Victoria. I'm here. We were supposed to meet today."

"Yes, Victoria..." he cleared his throat, "...didn't you receive our letters?"

"Letters?"

"Hold on. Give me a second, and I'll be right there to let you in."

What letters? She gave them one address; there should be absolutely no reason why she wouldn't receive their mail.

Sweet Victory

The door nearest her sprang open automatically. Tony stood on the inside. No smile or greeting. She extended her hand. "Hi, Tony."

"Victoria. I wish I would have known you hadn't received any of our letters."

A nervous rumble boiled in Victoria's stomach. "This sounds like something important." There were only a few weeks before the Beale Street Music Festival would take place. She didn't have time for any detours.

"Come inside, and I'll explain."

Less and less of an explanation was needed with each step Victoria took. The employees that had been bustling through the building on her previous visits were nowhere to be seen. Instead, they'd been replaced by contractors wearing uniforms displaying company names and logos. Some installed new equipment in the kitchen areas, some scrubbed ceramic tile floors, and even more worked in the bathroom areas.

Tony motioned toward a seat at a small conference table. "Have a seat, Victoria."

She stood glaring down at him. "Tell me what's going on."

"It's really routine. We received an inspection that was not favorable."

"Not favorable?"

"Yes, in fact, we failed."

"When I visited, and signed my contract everything was fine."

"Yes, but we receive inspections on a regular schedule."

"So, what does this mean?" Anger crept into her voice. "If you knew this would happen, then why weren't you better prepared, and why didn't you call when you received no response from the letters?"

"The letters weren't returned, and there were explicit instructions about deadlines and alternative options. We just assumed..."

"You assumed. Great," she flopped into a chair in front of her, "So, what is your current status?"

"We took this as an opportunity to upgrade a few other things, as I'm sure you noticed. We'll have everything inspected again in a week, but I am not sure if that gives you enough time for what you need."

"Not sure." Victoria rocketed out of her seat. What did he mean...not sure. She'd sunk all of her money into this plan. His company had a deposit check from her that would allow her to take care of herself and Gramps for about six months. According to Corey, there were no bites on the townhouse, but she didn't really know if he was trying. It was listed, but no offers had been placed. "What about my money? The contract says ninety days in an event of God or I cancel, but you failed an inspection."

He stared at her from the opposite side of the table. Shaky fingers raked across his bald chocolate scalp. A quick removal, inspection, and replacement of his glasses followed. Then, he continued, "Yes, but per the contract we notified you, and now we have ninety days to get your money back to you minus expenses."

"What expenses?"

"Anything we would have purchased in an effort to make your project run smoother."

She began to pace the room. "What did you purchase for my project?"

"We leased mixers and packaging for pies and cakes."

"What did that cost?"

"I don't have pricing in front of me, but the information

was in the letters."

"I didn't receive any letters from you or your company. Why didn't someone call?"

"Victoria, I guess this is sort of sudden for you, but..."—after scribbling something down, he handed her a piece of paper—"...these are the names of three companies, smaller, but good that might be able to help you."

She snatched the paper from his hands. Why would she want any contacts he gave her? She had a little more than two weeks to figure out what to do or she'd lose the money she deposited to hold her place in the festival, as well as part of the money she'd given him. God, why did she even try to make this work?

She should've just taken a job.

"Thanks. I'll consider it. And I want the equipment returned immediately to the vendor that you leased from. The packaging I will take with me, now." She wrote her address down on a piece of the paper he'd given her, ripped it off, and handed it to him. "Please have someone from your company mail verification to me of returned equipment, packaging costs, and expected date of receipt for my deposit. I believe you are in breach of our contract. Although you mailed a notice, still you are not able to fill our agreement in the manner we contracted. If necessary, I will hire a lawyer to pursue this further. You have two weeks."

Victoria dragged herself into the home she shared with her grandfather hours later tired and upset. The companies Michael had listed were spread from Bartlett, Tennessee to Southhaven, Mississippi. No contracts were signed because she didn't want to spend the money, again. Only a couple of weeks remained before the Beale Street Music Festival. Even if she could figure out how to make it through that event, what would she do about the actual barbeque battle? If she wanted to sell her desserts, she needed someplace to be able to package them in order to fulfill order requests, and supply A&R Barbeque. *If she received any orders.* God, how did she get here?

She tossed her keys on the table next to the door, and picked up the mail. The envelope in her hand ripped to shreds as she tore it away from the letter it concealed. She glanced back at the front of the envelope...forwarded. Tony's secretary had sent the freaking letter to her address in Maryland. Why? Crap. Her driver's license. The secretary used the address from her license instead of what she wrote on her forms.

Someone opened the letter, then stuffed it inside of another envelope, and sent it to Memphis. Anger crawled over her entire body. "Ahhh," she yelled. "Damn it! Corey." Why would he read it, know its importance, and wait so long to send it to her? Why not call her? He knew there was a deadline.

Gramps shuffled into the living room as she raced toward the telephone. She'd dialed most of it when he asked, "What's going on?"

"Oh, Gramps...I don't know what I was thinking." The tattered pieces of paper in her hands shook from anger. "And, now this. I don't have enough money to find another packager."

"What happened?" Soft house shoe clad feet padded across the room, and stopped beside her. "Were you calling Mikey?"

"No, I was calling Corey. For some reason, he didn't call me when these papers," she shook the ripped pages in her hand at Gramps, "came to the house. If I would have known earlier, I probably could have figured something out..."

Gramps sat the phone back in its receiver, and pulled her to the couch with him. Soft wrinkled hands held hers. She focused on the brown spots on the back of them that didn't used to exist.

"What are those papers about?"

"They're about the packager. They failed an inspection, but since I didn't know about it...my money is wrapped up with them."

"What would you have been able to do?"

"I don't know, but something...get the money back so that I could use it elsewhere."

"How long will it take them to give your money back?"

The couch cushions gave in to her weight as she sank deeper into them resting her head back. She slid her hand from Gramps, and made air quotes with her fingers. "Ninety days, and they say they've got to make deductions for some things they purchased because they hadn't received a response from me about anything."

"Hmm, it seems we've got to figure out another way." He sat back, crossed his legs, propped his elbow on his thigh, and rested his chin on a tiny fist. "I think we should call Mikey, and think through this together." Again, he picked up her hand, and cradled it between his own. "Don't worry Victory, we'll find an answer."

"Gramps, I think I need to face the fact I wasn't ready for this. I need to try to take a job, and quickly. We don't have a lot of money left." For a moment, she closed her eyes, and then opened them to find his staring back. "Gramps, we might have to move."

"Okay, we can sell the house, and find a little apartment somewhere."

He thought she meant move down the street, but she meant move to wherever she could find a job. "Gramps, we might have to leave the area. There aren't many jobs here that fit my skills."

"Move away from Memphis? Victory, what about

Mikey?"

Shame filled her, but what was she going to do? She'd made a promise to Mikey, but she had to find a way to take care of herself and Gramps. At seventy-six, he was doing well, but she'd noticed some days seemed a little harder than others for him. There were days when his appetite was not as hardy. And he refused to let her take him to a doctor for the really good checkup. Taking care of someone his age required special training, and time. Time that she had less and less of. Her head dropped into the palms of her hands. "I don't know, Gramps."

Butterflies flitted about in her stomach. Not the good kind, but the 'I-don't-know-what-I'm-going-to-do kind'. En route from work, Mikey had no idea she would tell him she needed to consider moving out of state. A few recruiters had emailed about a couple of possibilities in Nashville and Atlanta. She didn't want to go back to Maryland. Nashville and Atlanta weren't far, she and Mikey could try the long distance thing for a while. Maybe, in time, she could find a worthwhile position in Memphis or he could come to her. They may have to wait until Paige is older, but something could be done. She knew it.

Later, as she laid in bed the click and scratch of the key in the lock awakened her butterflies. Even though she knew he tip-toed so he wouldn't wake Gramps, each footstep thudded with the beat of her own heart.

As his eyes crawled over her body, a smile crept onto his face erasing the tiredness. Fishnet covered her body, well, if you could consider the amount of her body touched by the fishnet *as* covered. She rose from bed, and walked toward him allowing him to take in the full visual affect of the red strands wrapping her body. He reached for his belt, removed it, placed his gun in it's usual place in the closet, and waited. Each step closer broadened his smile.

Sweet Victory

"Baby, you look beautiful." When she was within reach, his hands caressed every inch of her body. His hold on her tightened, and he pulled her so close her form puzzled against the curves of his hungry body perfectly. The bulge pressing against her body told her what his words didn't. He dipped his head into the bend of her slender neck, and licked an exposed piece of skin. "You taste like honey." His hands slid across her bottom, pressing her body even more tightly to his.

One hand snaked between the two of them, and then moved between her legs. Realizing there was nothing keeping his fingers from the most intimate parts of her his eyes widened. He removed his hand and hurriedly unzipped his pants. The tip of his penis slid inside of her with no further warning. With his hands supporting her butt, he lifted her, and she wrapped her legs around his torso. Although he filled her, she craved more. She slid along the length of his shaft, hungry for each stroke. When their bodies joined at the center she couldn't resist tightening her legs around his waist, and taking all of him into her.

"Victory..."

Her mouth covered his. Nibbles and kisses prevented him from speaking. His essence filled her as she inhaled. The urge to give everything inside of her to him overflowed. "I love you."

He stopped, and kissed her gently. "I love you, too."

She wanted to cry, but she didn't. Softly, their bodies clapped as he pumped her up and down his shaft. She moaned in complaint as he paused to walk toward the bed she'd rested in waiting for him. Together, they fell to the bed breaking his rhythm for a second. Then, he shifted her legs so the back of her thighs pressed against his arms, and he eased into her again. Each thrust brought her closer to ecstasy. His tongue traced a path from her legs to her breasts flicking at the strands of fishnet. Teeth brushed

134

across her nipples as his fingers tore at the netting covering them. Strings of shredded fabric lay across her body. Nothing impeded him as his mouth covered her nipple, and his tongue played, hardening the tip until she thought she would burst into flames from her own longing. Each time their bodies joined, he placed tender kisses along her neck. When he reached her lips, the kiss she returned was sad, remorseful. Her soul twisted into knots. Tears rolled down her face as she felt her body reach its climax, and his body pulse inside her. He let her legs fall from his arms, and he attempted to rise, but she held on, tightly.

He searched her eyes for something, then she closed them, and softly he kissed each eyelid. "Why are you crying?"

"I miss you already."

"Why? I'm right here."

He attempted to rise again. She rolled onto her side, and curled up against him, resting her head on his chest. "Don't." It was the only word she could manage before her throat closed. If she attempted to say anything more, she'd tell him about moving, and she didn't want to tell him anything, not yet. There might still be another way.

"Baby, let me pull off this uniform. "

"Please don't."

Again, he searched her eyes. This time, she doubted he found the answer he hoped for, but he gave her what she wanted, and laid beside her. She fell asleep in his arms where she knew she would be loved until morning.

Chapter Fourteen

The sun rose, but didn't shine. Nothing seemed clear on the wintry March day. Mikey had poked around all day before leaving for work. She'd cooked, cleaned, and occupied herself with whatever she could in order to avoid having any sort of real conversation. When nothing else worked, she teased him with kisses and promises of more when he returned from work. He didn't push her for answers, and left with questions.

As soon as he left, she picked up the phone and called Corey. The sound, expectation, of his voice angered her even more. It was as if he'd been waiting on her call.

"Victoria. Hi."

Why respond to his cursory greeting. She wanted to launch herself like a missile through the phone right at him. "Corey, why did you hold onto my paperwork? I know you saw that it was important."

"Important? How was I to know that?"

"You opened and read it. It requested a return phone call. It said I'd be liable for expenses after a certain date." Her annoyance and anger increased with each word.

"Victoria. What are you doing down there? Throwing your money into desserts? That's a waste."

There it was; his reason. Even a thousand miles away, he wanted to control her and what she did. "Why are you worried about what I'm spending my money on?"

"Because I miss you. I want us back."

What! There had to be some sort of angle with Corey. He'd never admit such a thing without being able to get something out of it. "What do you want?"

"What do I *want*?"

"Yes." *And for God's sake, be honest.*

"I want you to come back home, and stop playing games. It's been long enough."

"I'm not coming back to you." She might have to move somewhere, now, thanks to him.   But, she would never go back to him. "Even if I move." *Why did she say that?*

She imagined a smile crossing his face. "So, you have been thinking about coming home?   Good."   Some sort of indiscernible chatter in the background interrupted them.

"No...I'm not moving back..."

"I'm coming down. We can talk about this more then."

"Corey..."

"Listen.   There are things I think we should talk about face to face. If they don't interest you, then I'll leave, and..."

"And, what?"

There was a clicking sound.   "I've got to grab this line. See you soon."

"Corey, we need to talk. About the house..."

"I'll let you know when I'm flying in. I've got to go."

The conversation was over in classic Corey style.   He'd made his point, and nothing else needed to be said.   God, what did he mean by *soon*?   She had too much to deal with, and didn't need Corey to add to her mountain of problems. The money from the sale of the house would help a lot, but could take a while.   Her share would give her and Gramps a lot more wiggle room.   If Corey wasn't coming to hand her a check, she didn't need to see him. Tomorrow, she promised herself she'd shoot him an email or text to clarify why he was coming down, but for now, she needed to focus on applying to jobs just in case.

The day dragged along until Mikey returned from work. He'd decided to work overtime in order to make a few extra dollars toward Paige's tuition, she guessed. At 1:00 A.M., her heavy eyelids only remained open because of a pot of coffee she'd guzzled an hour earlier. Relief washed over her body when she heard the twist of the bedroom doorknob. She didn't have a real plan, but she needed to tell him there was a strong possibility she would be leaving after the music festival. Whatever job she found, she'd take.

She sat up in bed, and watched his usual routine: belt, gun, closet. He kissed her on the cheek, and began to undress. "Babe, I can't believe you're still awake."

"I wanted to wait for you."

He yawned. "What's on your mind?" He continued to undress and she watched. It was a present being opened: shirt, vest, t-shirt, and pants. She waited from him to remove the rest, but he stopped. "Babe, what's on your mind?"

She looked up to see him staring at her. Everything she'd been holding inside the past days from the packager to Corey poured out of her. When she finished she was in tears, held together only by Mikey.

"Why didn't you tell me? Why the secrets?"

"I wanted to see if I could figure out another way, but I can't. Everything I think of involves money, and I don't have any more. What's left needs to be spent on making sure Gramps has a place to stay." Watery hazel eyes scanned the walls of the room around her. "He wants me to sell this house, but I can't. I'm going to rent it, and find us a place wherever I have a job offer." She paused again. "Maybe, I should've entered that SBDC business plan contest, huh?" she joked.

He didn't respond to her attempt at humor. "So, you planned all this without asking me for help?"

"You've got so much on your plate already. Paige's tuition, your own place..."

His head fell down to rest on top of hers. "That's part of my point."

"What?"

"Victory, there's enough room here for both of us, and a spare room for Paige, and she knows and loves Gramps."

"I can't ask you to put your life on hold for me and Gramps."

The warmth of his arms disappeared, and he pulled away from her. She straightened to look up at him.

"Put my life on hold. Is that really what you think I'd be doing?"

"I don't...I..."

"You know I love you, and being with you is what I want. What do *you* want?"

"I want to be with you, too, but I don't know what to say to all of this." She'd just spent the last how many years living with a man, and what did it get her? Of course, she knew Corey and Mikey where completely different people, but 'playing house' with another man wasn't something she thought she was ready for. Even if she did need the financial help.

"You're still busy trying to run away from you and me. Why?"

"I'm not running away from anything. I just want you to be sure..." *God, nothing is coming out right.*

"I was sure twelve years ago."

"I love you, and I want to be with you, but can I think

about it? I want to discuss it with Gramps."

His head leaned against the headboard, and a hand wiped across his forehead. "Think about it. Discuss it with Gramps, but this time Victory if you leave, I won't be here when or if you come back." He rose from the bed, and returned to the closet. For a moment, he stood with his back to her, and then he turned to stare at her. "You need to figure some things out." Everything he removed earlier, he put back on.

Words he'd never said before sank into every cell of her body. If there was ever a next time, returning to Tennessee would mean nothing. Because if she did, he wouldn't be waiting or accepting of her when she returned. And even though she hadn't thought about it before, she had to admit a part of her knew the moment she looked up at him on the road her first night back in Tennessee that she'd returned for more than her grandfather.

The weeks leading up to the Music Festival were lonelier than she'd expected. Mikey had given her space she hadn't expected to, "...think and discuss..." with Gramps. She'd been on her own to visit her site, to design her signage, to negotiate with the vendors for pricing for product, and to set-up things with the new packager. She didn't want to waste a lot of money on a contract like she'd had with the last one, so she was only going to use them for the festival, and then, if she needed it, she'd find some place cheaper. But, she needed money from the sale of the house, her refund from the other packager, or a job before she could make any further decisions.

Chapter Fifteen

Warm water rained down on Victoria. As her hands slid across warm wet tiles, tangled locks covered her eyes, but did not hinder the stream of tears as they mixed with the rapid hard flow of water. Maybe the water could wash away the events of the past few days.

A slow tremble traveled through her body, and her legs began to fold beneath her. She reached out to grab something. As her fingers gripped and tightened on the shower curtain, the plastic tore from the metal rings. With each snap and pop, she slid further down the wall behind her until her bare bottom rested on the tub. At first, she tried to get up, but then she sat. Why get up?

Everything and everyone seemed to be trying to push her down. Her ex-bosses. Corey. Her new business. In her watery confessional, she replayed the crazy events of her life.

Walter Davies—VP of Excel—walked into her office, and changed her life. His expression was odd. "Did I disturb you?" His pale skin seemed a little paler if that was possible. Dark circles created an odd raccoon affect around his eyes, and his glasses only seemed to enhance it. Victoria always thought Walter would make the perfect Santa at the office holiday parties, but not that day.

"No, you're not bothering me. Have a seat. I expected John, but since he hasn't arrived, what can I do for you?"

Sweet Victory

They both sat. Walter removed his jacket, and tossed it over the back of his chair. Sweat stains marked the underarms of what at some point had been a crisp white shirt. His hands slid up and down his thighs for a moment, and then he spoke.

"I just left John's office. He should be joining us shortly, but I wanted to come and speak with you first." He paused, and looked into Victoria's eyes. Then he began again. "I don't know how much you've heard, but last year was rough. As a result, we've got to cut $500,000 out of the budget."

At that moment, jean clad John Thomas entered her office with a bagful of popcorn. "Sorry I'm late, but I was stuck on the phone. He sat in one of the available chairs at the conference table in her office, and waited.

Walter continued. "As I was saying, because of the economy we've had to make a lot of cuts. We've examined everything, and we think that your department is a little heavy."

Victoria felt her stomach do flips. What was he saying? This could not be happening. Her department only had five people. What would her employees do? "Walter," her head sprung back and forth, "John. My team is one of the smallest in the company. We've got ten offices located throughout Maryland, Virginia and DC, and my team handles the staffing needs for all of them. We're stretched thin enough as it is." She couldn't think of anyone who she could or would want to let go.

John sifted through the popcorn, leaned back his head, and threw a fistful of kernels in his mouth. After munching for a considerable length of time, he spoke. "We've estimated that if you can get your department down to three people, and take a cut yourself of say...about twenty-five percent that would be a great help."

"Lay off two people?" She couldn't believe what she

was hearing. "Take a pay cut?" A pay cut would definitely change her lifestyle, but she'd squirreled away most of her bonus checks for the past eight years. "If taking a pay cut means saving my staff, yes, but if not which two would you suggest I fire? Mrs. Peterson has worked for this company for ten years organizing employee training and development. Jeffrey for three years has coordinated all employee relations, performance management, and policy administration. Brandon is the only analyst we've ever employed. He spent every day analyzing cost and utilization researching vendor relations in an effort to improve that data. And Crystal, she's improved our payroll processing over previous years, and maintains all of our personnel files single-handedly." Her hand lifted to her temple. The pressure she applied didn't ease the sting behind her eyes. "We haven't increased our budget one dime over last year."

Mrs. Peterson's husband passed away a year ago, what would she do without her job? Would her kids have to take care of her? Jeffrey and his wife just had a new baby girl. Crystal was fresh out of college, and eager to learn everything. She had an incredibly bright future ahead of her. Although she had a roommate, and could easily replace her salary, a layoff might crush her spirit. Tony had no degree, but a lot of heart. He was a young man that worked hard for his company, and expected his company to do the same for him.

Walter stared at the side of John's head, and then looked back at Victoria. "Victoria, we know this is hard, but we need the cuts in order to keep everything else going forward."

"Yes, Victoria, we know this is hard, but we've got to cut the budget." With a shrug, John continued, "And, unfortunately human resources is an easy area we can cut." Again, Walter glared at John silently.

"Human resources is an area you can cut. What? John, the team I've put together works well. We've been able to handle all issues from lack of account managers to training to new site openings without any problems. And I've even developed new methods to assist us with our diverse candidate searches and placements."

Victoria realized the plastic curtain was still twisted between her fingers as she sat thinking about Walter and John. She couldn't believe they'd sat in front of her speaking about her department and staff as if they were inconsequential. It's true Excel wasn't where she thought she would be when she graduated from college. Her degree in business management hadn't landed her her dream job. Honestly, she didn't even know what that was anyway. The degree framed on the wall in her basement had simply been a way out of Tennessee.

A temp agency had actually placed her in her first job with her first company—only company, and kept her from going back. They liked her (she thought), and she was good at what she did, so she did it. She hadn't gone back to school for her masters, because she hadn't need it. She was making six figures, and received bonus checks of twenty percent of her income. It allowed her to do everything she wanted: travel, drive a nice car, own a nice condo, and pay for her grandfather's nursing home. It's not like she had children or a family. John might think her department was an easy cut, a quick fix to a bad budget, but she knew that each member of her team was important. And each, for their own reasons, needed their jobs and their income. She released the torn plastic in her hand, and curled into a tight ball resting her head against the wall behind her, as she continued to replay the memories.

"We appreciate all that you and your team have done," Walter had said.

"Walter, tell me, what about all of the premiums? Redskins tickets? Orioles tickets? Nationals tickets? Wizard tickets? Have those been cut?"

Walter shifted in his seat. John spoke, "We are still

reviewing those areas of the budget, but we have decided to cut back those, too."

"Cut back? Not cut out?" She kept her voice level, but inside she wanted to scream, and pound her fist on the desk. "John, we spend about $200,000 on those premiums alone."

"We are still evaluating the premiums, but we'll also make some changes in the health plan to assist with the budget cut." Walter added.

She was sure that any cuts to the health insurance would work against the staff, too. "How long do I have to think about this?" she asked.

"We need you to do this as quickly as possible. Can you put it all together over the next two to three weeks," said John.

Victoria placed her elbows on the table, and steepled her fingers underneath her chin. "Are you guys giving me anything to offer my team?"

Walter responded. "As long as your suggestions are within reason."

There was nothing more she could say. Other departments had much larger staffs than hers. John and Walter had made their decision, and she couldn't change their minds.

She'd grabbed her purse, and stormed out of her office seconds after them. The only place she could think to go was home. For a brief moment, it had been her haven, but then the click of the lock, and twist of the front door knob washed away that calm. Her stomach reeled, and for some unknown reason, she fussed with her hair and clothing. Then she leaned back onto the chaise and took a quick sip of wine.

Corey, her boyfriend of the last three years walked in. "Hey." Paul Mitchell's entire collection of product molded Corey's perfectly sculpted curls in place. Flawless pecan colored skin and charcoal curls hinted at his Trinidadian heritage. The expensive fabric of the black suit he wore still showed signs of being freshly pressed at the cleaners. The perfect salesman. Who could say no to him?

He dropped his keys on the table, leaned down to kiss her on the cheek, and kept going to the bedroom. Over his shoulder he yelled, "How was your day?"

His words were empty. Just the normal routine question people asked at the end of the day.

No matter what she'd said, the conversation would be tough. So, she might as well just dive in. "I have to lay off two people, and take a pay cut." Shaky hands lifted her wine glass to her lips. His footsteps stopped. Her breath caught in her throat. The leather bottom of his shoes skipped a beat on the hard wood floor as he turned around and walked back toward the living room.

Even though he was angry, his well-rehearsed expression never changed. No frown. No raised voice. Nothing. Always picture perfect. Except for the barely noticeable color change in his cheeks. "What pay cut? Why? When?"

"Yeah, pay cut." Her own demeanor did not mirror his. A slight uncontrollable pitch raised her voice. "Budget cuts. In the next two or three weeks."

"So, why don't you lay off three people or give more people pay cuts, then you won't have to take one?"

Victoria choked on a mouthful of wine. She sat her glass on the wood table beside her, and patted her chest with a hand. "What? You've met all of my staff before. You know their families. How could you say that?"

"What? You're concerned about them? What about us? What about our household? Owning a six bedroom townhouse in Fairfax County isn't exactly easy."

"We can cut back. We don't...don't have any kids."

Her arms stretched out in front of her.   "We don't need a townhouse this big."

"So, I have to change my life because you don't want to give your staff pay cuts.   You're being selfish.   What about me?"

She scooted to the edge of the chaise, and fixed her gaze on the man she loved.   Tears trickled down her laugh lines dripping from her chin into her wine glass.   What she needed him to say, he didn't.

He tugged at the tie around his neck loosening it, and unbuttoned the top button.   "Yeah, you think about it.   You think about us, too.   Think about what's important to you."

Victoria crawled out of the tub, and wiped at the condensation covering the mirrors in her bathroom.   The eyes staring back showed her weariness.   That day hadn't been easy, but the possibility of having to decide to leave Mikey was harder.

She knew what was important to her, but how did she keep from losing it all?

"I don't know, Myles."   Chad sat squished in the passenger seat of the squad car next to his partner puzzled. "I know she loves me, but I don't seem to be able to get her to trust me."

"You don't think she trusts you?"   Now, Myles looked confused.   "Man, after all you two have been through...do you really think it's about trust?"

"She told me she needs to think and discuss my moving in with Gramps..." he lowered the volume of the scratchy voice booming across the radio.   "Doesn't she think I

Sweet Victory

would've given her that time, and we could've discussed it with him together?"

"Does she talk a lot about her past or why she came back?"

"No, not really, but I know a lot of crazy bull went down, but that's not me. Not us."

"I'm not saying that...I'm just saying maybe she's just a little gun shy."

"Maybe, but when does she just follow my lead..."

Shots rang out. Tires squealed. A royal blue Crown Vic peeled out; turning the corner at the end of the block. A familiar Pocahontas plat floated in the wind out the driver's side window. Tennessee tags Charlie Echo...

"Shit...Myles. You okay? Myles."

Chad grabbed the radio. "Officer shot. Need assistance at the corner of Lamar and American Way." He focused on Myles again. "Send ambulance. Look out for royal blue Crown Vic, female driver, TN tags, first two: Charlie Echo, headed north on Getwell."

As the dispatcher called out all resources...he ripped through Myles' clothes searching for damage. Quickly, his hands were covered in blood. The car door and seat took a few of the bullets, but at least two had hit him in the thigh, and one in the lower stomach. He applied pressure to the wound on his partner's side, but the blood from all of the wounds was too constant. Damn. Where was that back up?

Every squad car from his district showed up...blocking off every inch of the neighborhood, only allowing entrance of the ambulance. As his partner was strapped onto a gurney, and loaded into the back of the ambulance, he made plans to find Jamal Echols and his mysterious female friend.

Chapter Sixteen

The freaking legs of the stool Victoria stood on sank into the soft muddy earth, again.   The tent pole slipped from her hands, and she fell.   God, this was tedious, she wiped her muddy hands on her pants, and tried again.

Tom Lee Park was the perfect location for the Beale Street Music Festival.   The Mississippi Bridge hid in the foggy horizon of the sunrise, only its lights shone through; the perfect setting for a Stephen King thriller.   Scents of barbeque: cinnamon, peppers, garlic floated through the air over the brown waters of the Mississippi as they lapped against the banks at a steady lazy pace in rhythm to B.B. King's guitar piping through the sound system.   Squinting, she raised her face to the sky, if only the rain would stop, it might not be such a bad day.

Without Mikey, she'd had to hire a few temps to help her. They were busily working away on setting up the outside awning.   She focused on everything else: menus, merchandising of her product, and cleaning.   With so little money, she couldn't afford to rent the type of unit she'd really needed, so she decided not to cook at this event, just sell.   At this point, she didn't know what sleep was, but she had a ton of product on-hand.

By noon the coffee she'd been drinking was no longer having much of an effect on her.   Although the music festival was the kick-off, the numbers of people wandering around surprised her.   All of Memphis, and the nearby areas where there.   Television cameras from all of the local news channels were set-up throughout the grounds.   The Food Network, and a few other cable channels she didn't recognize were there, too. Maybe she could get lucky, and one of them would interview her.

She checked on everything with Tanya and Lisa, her temps for the day, and then she retreated for a quick minute into the trailer before ducking out.   She wanted to walk around and grab a few samples of *real* food.   If one more piece of cake or pie crossed her lips, she'd blow up five dress sizes.   The succulent tangy A&R rib tip she was wolfing down wouldn't help her cause, but it was delicious, almost as good as it tasted on Mikey...   The memory instantly pained her.   *Why?* Because it was one more thought of time spent with him.   Time she might never have again.

"Hungry?"

The snarky tone in the voice startled her.   "Rebecca." She scanned the crowd to see who was with her, but she didn't see anyone.   "Are you here for your committee work or for fun?"

She waved the clipboard in her hands.   "Somebody's got to make sure all of you are selling only what you are supposed to."   She leaned in and whispered as if they were conspirators or *friends*, "You know some people actually try to get over on us, and sell unapproved items."   Then she threw her head back, and laughed as if she had told the best joke in the world.

"Really?   Why don't they just get permission to sell the other items?"

"Because we don't want too many people selling the same ole same ole, so they tell us they're going to sell something different and great, and then when they see everyone is only buying one thing, they try to sneak it in."

"Ohh. I guess I get it."

"So, I passed by your stand, and I didn't see Chad. I thought he was working with you. I didn't have the other ladies' names on my list."

God, that's all she needed right now, another Mikey war. "Is that a problem? I didn't see anything anywhere that said I couldn't change staff names."

"No, I was just wondering...you know with you two being *so* close, and all why he wasn't here."

"Rebecca, I don't think that's any of your business." The crowd around them seemed to grow within the moments they stood there. They were brushed up against, and pushed. The rib tip Victoria held was knocked to the ground, and a haphazard, "I'm sorry," followed. She stared at it on the ground, and thought those were some happy ants. "Anyway, Rebecca, don't worry about Chad and I, we're doing just fine."

"Really?"

"What do you want?"

"I just think it's funny."

"What?"

"In high school you left, and now, it looks like he's left you."

She turned to walk away. "Rebecca, I don't have time for you or your childish games any longer."

"Well, he had time for my games last night. When he slept at my house."

"What?" She spun around, and the quick movement caused her to lose hold of her plate of remaining food. *Crap.* The lines were super long, now; she wouldn't have time to get back into line to get anything else to eat. She'd have to ask one of the ladies to bring her something when she relieved them. "What do you mean when he slept at your

153

house?"

"What do you think I mean? You can't keep a man from the mother of his child." With that, Rebecca turned, and disappeared into the mash of people around her.

Victoria didn't remember her route back to her location, but the next time she blinked she was behind the front counter of her trailer again, and a crowd of clamoring customers was in front of her. *Maybe she hadn't brought enough.* They still had about five hours left in the night, and they'd sold nearly half.

Ms. Lisa emerged from the rear of the trailer with a plate of rib tips. She loved the kindly older woman even more than she had at 5:00 A.M., she'd requested the temps arrive at 6: 30 A.M., but Lisa had called the night before for directions, and when they spoke she mentioned she'd be there at 5 o'clock. Ms. Lisa volunteered to come early to help her set up, plug in, and get started. If this plan worked, Ms. Lisa was definitely hired.

Weak-kneed from hunger, she wobbled over to Lisa, hugged her, and dived into the rib tips. "Thank you, Ms. Lisa." Her mouth watered at the thought of the first bite. "God, these are so delicious." The rib meat melted on her tongue.

"Honey, you must be starving."

She glanced up from her plate to see Ms. Lisa staring at her with a huge smile.

"Oh my God, was I. I dropped my plate on the ground earlier."

"I wondered why you didn't have anything when you came back."

"We had such a huge crowd." She set her plate on a table, and turned back toward the front of the trailer. She'd left Tanya to fend for herself, but Tanya handled it well. She guessed Tanya could tell she was starved, too. "Tanya, we're on our way."

"Don't worry 'bout it Ms. Victoria. I can handle it."

She hated to take advantage, but she really wanted to finish eating.

"I'll go up front to help her." Ms. Lisa pulled up a stool for Victoria. "You sit right here, and relax."

She couldn't resist the offer. Without Mikey she'd done everything herself. Gramps had helped with some prep, but she had been a little cautious about allowing him to help. His color still didn't sit well with her, and he continued to refuse to go to the hospital. *Stubborn old man.* She bit into another rib tip. "Mmm."

"Ms. Victoria, you have a friend coming around back," said Tanya over her shoulder.

A friend. God, she did not feel like dealing with Rebecca again.

At the sound of a knock on the rear door, she reluctantly placed her Styrofoam container on a counter, and walked toward the back of the trailer. As soon as the door opened, a tiny bear hug latched around her waist. The mass of wiggling blond curls hid the face of her captor, but she knew her anyway. She scooped her up, and immediately her senses were overtaken with chocolate and soda.

"Hi, sweetie."

"Hey, Ms. Victoria. Where have you been?"

"I'm sorry I haven't seen you lately, but I've been trying to get things ready for today."

"That's what Daddy said, too, but now, you'll be back, right?"

"Hey, are you going to ask her a million questions?" asked Mikey from the other side of the door.

Sweet Victory

Victoria peered over Paige's shoulder into Mikey's eyes. She'd missed him, but what was she going to do about it. She kept making mistakes.   Paige slid out of her hug, and disappeared into the front of the trailer with Tanya and Ms. Lisa.

"Hi, do you want to come in?"

He peered inside the trailer at Paige.   "Is she okay up front?"

She looked back.   The ladies were fitting her with an apron, and she bubbled with excitement about helping with the customers. "Yeah, I think so."

"Then could you step out here?"

She stepped out of the trailer, and closed the door behind her.   Trash, generators, additional supplies surrounded them.   Not the ideal spot for an 'I'm sorry, please forgive' speech.   But, she might have to take her chance.

He raised his voice above the hum of the generators. "If you needed help, you could've called."

"I know."   But, what would that conversation have been like.   *I don't know what I want, yet, but could you come, and help me save my house, my grandfather...oh yeah, and me.*

"Do you need any help breaking down tonight?"

"Ms. Lisa called one of her sons, and Tanya called her brother."

"So, you don't need me to come back tonight?"

"I don't...I want..."

"Victoria, I'm simply asking if you need help."

She didn't, but she wanted him with her. "Yes.   Thank you."

Mikey reached around her, and grabbed the handle of the door. "I'll drop Paige off, and be back later."   With that, he entered the rear of the trailer, and returned with his smiling daughter. "Do you want to tell Victoria good night?"

Paige leaned away from her dad, and kissed Victoria on the cheek. "Good night, Ms. Victoria."

"Good night, sweetie."

Ms. Lisa' son, Tony, and Tanya's brother, Cliff, worked just as hard as they did.   They pulled trash, mopped, and scrubbed everything they saw.   The job market in Memphis had been just as tough as D.C., Tony had been laid off, and Cliff had only recently taken a job with a local bread manufacturer.   Tony had decided to use the option of attending college for free while receiving unemployment.   If she could, she'd offer them all jobs.   For tonight, she'd agreed to pay Tony and Cliff $10 per hour, which wasn't much, but for a few hours it could at least fill their gas tanks.

The step stool wobbled beneath her feet as she stretched in an effort to reach the latch holding her awning against the trailer.   She threw out her arms to steady herself, but the arm wrapped around her waist is what stopped her from falling.

"Do you always fall off things when I'm not looking?"

For absolutely no reason, she leaned against the man behind her.   Mikey.   The feel of his body against hers had been missed.

"Ms. Victoria, are you okay?" asked Tanya.

"Yes."   She glanced over her shoulder at Mikey.

Sweet Victory

"Thank you."

"What do you do when I'm not around?"

"Get my car stolen."

His arm slowly pulled away from her, and she stepped down off the step stool.

"What do you need me to do?"

He barely even looked at her. It felt like the most important thing all of a sudden. To have him look at her. To have him kiss her. "Can you help me load these boxes..."—she pointed at the awning—"...and then we can tackle that."

She doesn't even know how much time passed, but every dumb *girlie* thing she could think to do, she did. She blinked so much, she couldn't keep up with his movements, she flung her hair around to the point where she had a cramp in her neck, and if she tried to switch any harder she'd throw something out.

He shifted a few things around in the trunk of her car to accommodate another box, and clicked it shut. As he walked in her direction, he asked "Did you twist your ankle or something?"

At least he was watching. "No."

He glided past her to the awning. Without the aid of the step stool, he unlocked the latches, pulled it down, and stuffed it back into its container. It'd taken Tanya and Ms. Lisa an hour to get that thing right. He took it apart without a thought. The six foot tall standalone banners she'd ordered, he unhooked from their anchors, rolled up, and locked into their cases. She wasn't a tiny woman, but she'd needed to lean it and have Ms. Lisa hold it while she pulled and hooked it onto the anchor.

"Victoria, we're all finished inside. Do you need anything else?" asked Ms. Lisa.

"Thank you. I think everything is fine." She left Mikey stuffing banners into cases, and walked over to Ms. Lisa and her son. After grabbing her purse, she handed Tony cash, and signed off on Ms. Lisa's time card. Then she did the same thing with Tanya and Cliff.

A chorus of thank yous and good nights accompanied by hugs and waves ended their evening together.

She returned to Mikey. "Thank you for helping tonight. I think I can get the rest of this stuff into my car alone.

"Victoria, I don't have a problem helping you."

"I don't want to..."

"Victory, stop." He dropped the case he had in his hands, and filled his hands with her. "I'm tired. Why are you always playing games?"

"I'm not playing games."

"So, you think it was fine to just drop off the grid?"

She couldn't really think because his hands slid up and down her arms. The warmth the trail created heated her entire body from the inside out.

"I didn't 'drop off the grid'."

"What would you call it Victory? I haven't heard anything from you."

The warmth he created disappeared with the loss of his touch. She wrapped her arms around herself. "I gave you space."

"No, Victory. I gave *you* space. I wanted an answer. Answers."

"Mikey, I've...I've lived with a man before."

"I know that."

Words in her head jumbled, but she might as well say

159

them all. "No. I mean, I don't want to just live with another man." Her hands fell to her side, and she walked up to him. His hands were fisted in his pockets, but she stuffed her hands between his torso, and his arms, and wrapped them around him. "Even if that man is you."

At her last word, his body stiffened, and he tried to pull away, but she held on.

"No, Mikey, listen. For too many years, I lived and *thought* I loved a man who didn't love me. Not really." She angled her head back so she could see his face. That freaking basketball blank stare greeted her. "In his own way, I guess, but never enough to put me or my needs first. And I guess part of it is my fault because I never asked him to. And with Gramps and Paige..."

He reached around to where her hands clasped, and pulled them apart.

She kept talking. "And what about Rebecca? She told me you two were together...

He turned and walked away.

The last words of her sentence could only be heard by her. She's not even sure if she said them or not. "...last night."

The pressure on her chest forced the air out of her lungs. She leaned against the back of her car to stop from crumbling to the ground. *Mikey was gone.* He walked away from her. Left her in the middle of freaking Tom Lee Park. Her head fell into her hands, and tears streamed through her fingers.

She jumped at the sound of someone approaching from behind. 1:00 A.M in the middle of a park after of a full day of people partying and drinking, what was she thinking? She headed for the drivers' seat.

"Victory."

"Mikey?"

She paused at the door, and he stopped at the headlight.

"Victory, I don't need to hear about how another man loved you in his own way or any way. And Rebecca, why do you keep listening to her? I brought Paige home late because she was sick, and she didn't want me to leave. So, I slept in a chair in *her* room all night."

"I'm sorry..."

"Let me finish. For a long time, I've known what I wanted. I thought in time, you'd figure it out, too, and we...we'd be together..."

"Mikey..."

"Listen...you remember Jamal Echols?"

"Yeah."

"The night we arrested him, he was with a woman. That woman, his sister, did a drive by on our squad car the other night."

"Oh my God, Mikey." She threw her body into his. Tears poured down her face. "Mikey, why didn't you tell me? I've been acting like a child. I'm sorry. I...I was scared." She could've lost him, for good. "Is your partner okay? Have you found the woman?"

"Yes. She shot a cop in Memphis. Nobody slept, and then Paige got sick."

God, he was taking care of everyone, and no one was taking care of him. "Mikey, this is so unbelievable." She didn't know what to say. Her hands tightened around him, she wanted to protect him from everything, including herself.

His hands fisted in her hair, and pulled her head back so that he could look into her eyes. "I'm fine, but my partner was hospitalized. He's okay, but it made me think even more about what's important to me.   I never wanted you to *just live with me."*   He reached into his pocket, and pulled out a ring.   Not just a ring.   The ring his mother used to always clean, and only wear on special occasions when they were kids. His grandmother's ring.

In the early morning hours, nothing but darkness, the ring still shone bright.   Maybe the tears in her eyes helped, but it sparkled.

"Victory, I've loved you my entire life.   I lost you once, and I don't want to take the chance of losing you again."   He dropped one jean-clad knee to the muddy ground.   "I love you, and I want to marry you."   One hand held the ring out to her, the other slid up and down the back of her leg.   "Do you remember this ring?"

"Yes, but it looks a little different."

He smiled.   "I added four diamonds.   One for you, Paige...our baby, and me."

"Mikey..."

"I want us to begin our lives...our family.   Will you marry me?"

His stroke to the back of her knee or his words, she wasn't sure which, dropped her to her knees.   Their eyes locked onto each other, everything around them vanished into the background.   Her breathing synced with his.   A tear fell with each breath she took, not from sadness or pain, but from joy.   Her hand went to her chest; she opened her mouth to take in more air.

Gently, he touched his lips to her cheek.   "Baby, breathe."   He kissed the other cheek.   "Breathe."

Her breathing calmed, but the tears wouldn't stop. "Yes."

Chapter Seventeen

Paige was at her mom's, so, they'd taken advantage of having Mikey's apartment to themselves the entire night, but she wanted to tell Gramps the fabulous news. He'd bounce off the walls when he heard.

Mikey dropped her off at the house on his way to work. She raced through the house to Gramps' room. Knocked, and waited for an answer.

She placed her ear to the door. "Gramps." Knock. Knock. "Gramps." She checked her watch. "Gramps."

A queasiness roiled her belly. She twisted the knob, and slowly pushed the door open. For twenty seconds, her vision went black. She shook her head to clear her mind. Her legs wouldn't carry her fast enough, but she ran to the curled up figure on the floor.

Clothed in his robe, Gramps laid on the floor beside the bed with the smallest amount of vomit on his cheek. A bottle of pills dotted the floor around him. *I should've been here.* She felt for a pulse. Weak, but there. She grabbed the phone from his nightstand, and called 9-1-1.

"9-1-1." The slow southern drawl of the man on the other end was too calm.

"Yes, yes, my grandfather is injured."

"Where are you located?"

"2747 Gull Rd."

Sweet Victory

"Do you require assistance from law enforcement?"

"No, I think he passed out. I need an ambulance."

"Okay, ma'am. Calm down. Let me get a little more information. What happened?"

"I don't know. I came home, and I found him on the floor." She grabbed the pill bottle. *"It looks like he tried to take some aspirin."*

"Is he still conscious?"

"Yes, barely."

"Does your grandfather have a history of any conditions?"

"Uhh, no...nothing I know of." How could she not know the answer?

"What is your phone number?"

"555-1670. Please hurry."

"An ambulance is on its way."

She replaced the phone in its cradle, but then she picked it up again to call Mikey. She followed Mikey's instructions, and cleaned Gramps' face. Turned him onto his side, and stroked his back.

When the knock came, she bound from the bedroom to the door. The EMTs followed her to Gramps' room. Angry for not being at home, she hovered around the EMTs to make certain they didn't make a mistake because *she* already had.

She couldn't find her stupid cell phone, and she'd already locked the door. Running back inside, would just waste more precious time. A note would be the only way Mikey would know where they were until she could call from the hospital, besides he was on his way to the house. She scribbled *Regional Medical Center* onto a scrap of paper from her purse. Stuck the note between the door and the screen door, and ran to the ambulance.

Twelve years gone. Each freaking beep, and every tube kept telling her. Twelve years gone. She collapsed onto a chair next to a window in the small private room, and kicked off her shoes. The sweatshirt she wore belonged to Mikey. She pulled her arms out of the sleeves, and wrapped them around herself underneath the fabric. A mixture of cologne, laundry detergent, and *him* filled the air around her. She curled her legs up in the chair, and nestled into the sweatshirt more. She couldn't keep her eyes open.

"Victoria."

"Hmm. Mik..."—her eyes opened—"...ey."

Corey had just stepped off a plane, but he wore slacks and loafers. A tie. Always. He didn't have on a jacket, but there was probably one somewhere. No jeans. No sweatshirts.

"Who is Mikey?"

"Shh." She snuck a peek at her grandfather, and lowered her voice. "Corey, what are you doing here?" She stuffed her arms back into the sleeves, and stood. "Step outside. Gramps needs his rest."

Outside of the room, she leaned against the wall, raised her hands to her face, and swept them back over her hair detangling as she smoothed. Again, she asked, "What are you doing here?"

Corey grabbed her hand. Her hand with a new engagement ring. "What is this?"

She shook her hand free from his grip. "Let go of me," she said a little too loudly. Nurses, volunteers, doctors, visitors, and others paused to take in the scene. "Corey, I didn't invite you here. Please leave."

"Leave? I just got here, and it looks like just in time."

Sweet Victory

"I don't want to talk about this here."

"Then let's go outside.   You owe me some sort of explanation."

"No, I don't."

"Either you go outside with me or I'll stay up here with you."

A quick glance of the hallway, and she knew outside was the better place to have this conversation.

"You're getting on my nerves with this.   Come on, Corey."

The elevator took forever, the three floors down took longer.

Backed into a corner, in order to put space between the two of them, she fumed, "Corey, why did you come here?"

"I told you I was coming."

"You *told* me."   The ding of the elevator telling them it was time to get off saved him, and calmed her.   "I didn't take you seriously.   Outside, Corey, now."

He followed closely behind her.   In front of the hospital, he said everything that was on his mind.   You're here for a few months, and you're engaged."   He paced for a moment.   "What the hell is that about Victoria?"

"It's none of your business.   Why did you keep my paperwork, and what's going on with the house?"

"I didn't keep your paperwork.   I sent it to you.   And the house is not for sale."

"Not for sale?"

"No.   I came here to bring you back home."

"Back home."   She glanced up at the fourth floor windows of the hospital.   "This is my home."

"This place?"

"What do you mean? *This place?*"

"Come on Victoria, do you have a building over five stories? What jobs are here? What restaurants? Cultural events?"

"Why do you care?"

"Because I had a plan for us."

"You had a plan. What about what I wanted? How many years did you have me hanging around, waiting. Waiting for what?"

"It wasn't time, yet. I needed to make sure you were ready."

She wanted to kick something. "Make sure I was ready?"

"Yeah. Why would I want to marry somebody that didn't have anything?"

"That's why? You wanted me to have stuff."

"I wanted you not to need me. Have your own. Shit. I've dated a lot of women like that." In a somber voice, he continued, "Just trying to use a brother for everything."

She twisted the ring she wore in circles on her finger. "Did you think that's who I was? Some sort of freaking gold digger."

"No, but..."

"Victory." Mikey approached from behind her. "Baby, are you okay? How's Gramps?" He kissed her, and she kissed him.

"He's stable. Acute renal failure."

"Renal failure?"

"Yeah, his doctor said it was brought on by his blood

pressure medicine, age, and aspirin."

"What are they doing?"

"He's hooked up to a dialysis machine." Tears fell at the memory of her grandfather attached to the machine. Tubes in and out of his body. "The doctor said if the machine works he can prescribe some antibiotics and other medicines to get rid of extra fluid and keep his body balanced."

As she melted her body into his allowing his scent to fill her, and his warmth to comfort her, she remembered Corey. She took in a quick breath. "Mikey."

"Yes."

"I need to introduce you to someone."

He stepped back. Looked at her, and then at the suited up man across from them. His arms didn't leave her.

She spoke into his chest. "This is Corey."

"Corey."

Neither man extended a hand or gestured. They stared at each other, and then at her.

"Mikey, huh?"

"Call me Chad."

She hated to let go of him, but she needed to finish with Corey. "Baby, would you mind sitting with Gramps while he and I talk."

His grip tightened, then relaxed, and then it was gone. The touch of his kiss to her lips warmed her. "Which room?"

"412."

A cold breeze blew right through her reminding her that she only had on his sweater and some sweat pants with nothing underneath. Mikey disappeared inside of the building.   She grew colder, but the wind was no longer blowing.   He didn't stand around in the lobby watching or anything.   He went straight to the elevator without a glance over his shoulder.

"Corey, I don't know why things were so hard for us, but I don't care anymore."

"You don't care?"

"No.   I'm not mad, but I don't love you.   Not the way I should."

Corey leered in the direction of Mikey's path.   "Not the way you love him."

"It's not about him.   I thought I loved you..."

"You thought."

"I mean it felt like love...sort of."

"Sort of?"

"For so long, I didn't want anything.   Nothing, but you. When I needed you the most, you weren't there."

"I was there.   I tried to make sure you kept the job.   Do you know what it's like to grow up with nothing?"

"My family wasn't exactly rich."

"No, but your grandparents had a home, not the projects.   Not free lunches, food stamps and welfare."

"No, but..."

"But, nothing.   I didn't want to raise a family like that."

"Why didn't you tell me this years ago?"

"Because why did I need to?"

"Corey it would have made a difference."

"And now?"

She searched inside of herself.   The love she once had

Sweet Victory

was no longer there.

"My life is here."

He reached inside of his coat pocket. "I came to bring you this, too." He handed her a letter.

A letter from Excel. "What is this?" She flipped the envelope over. It had been opened. "You read it."

"Just read it."

She knew her mouth hung open. "This is why you called? Why you planned this whole surprise trip?"

"Like I said. To bring you back home."

Chapter Eighteen

"God, Corey, and to think...I..." Her words fell away as she ran through memories of the two them over their years together. *Had she always given him so much control? Why had she given up so much power over her own life?* Corey didn't think anything was wrong with what he'd done. It was how he'd handled everything in their relationship.

"We could have our lives back."

"Excel offered me my job back, so, you thought you'd just fly to Tennessee..."—she made a sweeping motion with her arms—"...and whisk me back."

"Victoria, you could use the money." He snatched the letter out of her hand. "They've even added a little extra."

"Extra."

"Yeah, they've been calling the house, too. I got them to kick in more. Couldn't you use the money for your grandfather?"

"I could, but...not like this, Corey."

"Then how?"

She was no longer able to control her anger. "You sell the house. Give me my half of the money," she yelled.

"I don't want to sell *my* house," he belted in return.

Stares from hospital patrons helped her calm her tone. "*Our* house. I need that money...like you just said, for my grandfather. For my life, here, in Memphis."

She didn't know what was going through his mind, but she watched as he seemed to be experiencing different emotions or thoughts. "Corey did you hear me?"

"I hear you. You need it for your life here, with *him*...I thought we were happier. That you were happier." He unfolded the letter, and read over it again. Then he handed it back to her. "If I don't hear from you by tomorrow morning, I'm leaving."

"Corey...I wasn't trying to hurt you."

He didn't stop; he continued to stalk toward a taxi waiting in the parking lot. She folded the letter, and stuffed it into her back pocket.

Mikey was sprawled across the chair she'd vacated earlier. She entered the room, but he didn't acknowledge her. There was no space for her to join him.

He moved to stand. "Here."

"No. I'm okay." She slid to the floor in front of him, and looped an arm around one of his legs. "I love you."

"Why was he here?"

"He wanted me to go back with him."

"What did he give you?"

"You saw that?"

He glanced around the room. "A wall full of windows, babe."

She reached into her pocket, and handed him the

folded envelope.   He read it, and asked "Your old life is waiting for you."   The letter fell to his lap.

"Yes."

"Him, too?"

"Yes."

"Uh huh."

"I have to go."   She hoped to pick up a check.   "Soon, I hope because the house should sell fast."

His fingers twisted in the curls of her hair.   "Do you still love him?"

She rose to her knees.   "I care, but I'm not in love him." She twisted around, and sank back onto the heels of her feet. "Insurance will cover most, but I just don't know how I'm going to pay for what's not covered, the bills, the business."

He picked up her hand, and kissed the ring he'd placed there.   "You mean we, right?"

"I love you."

He leaned over to her, and covered her mouth with his. "I love you more."

Someone clearing their throat interrupted them.

"Excuse us."

Mr. Kirkpatrick.   Mrs. Kirkpatrick.

"Mom.   Dad. What are you two doing here?"   He stood, and pulled her to her feet.

"Paige wanted us to bring her, but we told her we'd come, and let her know how Mr. James was doing," said Mrs. Kirkpatrick.

"I told her I'd call her back as soon as I knew something," said Mikey.

"You know your daughter," replied Mr. Kirkpatrick.

Sweet Victory

Victoria snuggled in closer to Mikey.

"Victoria, we're sorry to hear about your grandfather," said Mrs. Kirkpatrick. If we can help you with anything, please ask." She glanced at the ring on Victoria's finger, and smiled. "After all we're finally going to be family."

"Denise." Mr. Kirkpatrick nudged her.

"I'm sorry. I just..."

"No, it's okay, Mrs. Kirkpatrick."

At the sound of choking and gags, Victoria raced to her grandfather's side. "Gramps. We're going to get your doctor."

She glanced at Mikey, and he dashed into the hallway returning with a nurse, and Gramps' doctor.

"Mr. James, we're going to take care of everything. Just relax, and we'll see what we can do about getting you out of here, and back home with your family."

He reviewed Gramps' file, checked the dialysis machine, said something to the nurse in cryptic doctor speech, and then turned to Victoria and Mikey. "Your grandfather is strong. We will need to keep him here for a few days. Keep him on dialysis to let his kidneys rest. I've got him on antibiotics to prevent infection. As I said before, we'll also need to get rid of the extra fluid and keep his body's minerals in balance."

"So, he'll be okay."

"Well, we don't want to get ahead of ourselves. We'll need to change his diet, too. Limit sodium and potassium, among other things, but we'll tell you everything you need to know before he's ready to go."

"Thank you." Victoria couldn't stop herself from falling onto Gramps, and kissing every inch of his face. "Gramps, I thought I'd lost you."

Gramps cleared his throat. "No, sweetie. I couldn't leave you, now. I just got you back."

With her head resting softly on her grandfather's chest, she could hear his strong heartbeat. Much stronger than his soft scratchy words. "Gramps, I was so scared."

He raised a hand, and stroked her cheek. "Don't worry about me, Victory. I'm right here. Not going anywhere, sweetie. I hear there's gonna be a wedding," he smiled, weakly.

Epilogue

"Victory, we need more tea cakes up here," yelled Mikey over his shoulder.

"Coming right up." She grabbed a tray of tea cakes from the rack, and ran to the front of the trailer. "How many?"

After Gramps came home from the hospital, they used every moment of the two weeks to prepare for the Memphis in May Barbeque. Her email and voicemail had been flooded with call after call of order requests; they worked around the clock to fill them.

"Four."

"Here you go." As she handed him the four individually packaged tea cakes, she thought none of this would be possible without him.

He took the cakes from her. "Hey, is something wrong?"

"No." She placed the rest of the cakes on a rack near Mikey, and returned to the back of the trailer. From there, she watched. Mr. and Mrs. Kirkpatrick. Paige. Ms. Lisa, Tanya, Cliff, Tony take and fill orders. Gramps, too, but she made him sit on a stool. No standing for long periods or running around. He complained, but she knew he loved being fussed over.

"Hey, what are you doing?" asked Mikey.

"Nothing. Just thinking."

Sweet Victory

"About."

"You…"—she waved her arms around—"…this."

He walked over to her, and wrapped his arms around her. "Victory, you did it."

"Me. We. I never would've thought about using Gramps' church's kitchen instead of another distributor/packager." She snuggled a little closer.

"Gramps couldn't have been happier we used the kitchen, and that we'll be using the church in June." A smile broke out across his face, as he nuzzled his nose against the side of her cheek.

"I know." She pulled away for a moment to reach for her purse. "Look." She flashed a deposit receipt for him to review. "I got the money from the original packager. And Corey called to tell me we have a bid on the house. So, hopefully, there won't be any problems with the contract."

"So, now, you can make an honest man out of me."

"What. It's my reputation that's at stake here."

His breath floated across her skin. "Umm."

"How long do we have to be here?" He glanced over at all of the people buzzing around in the front of the trailer. "I think they can take care of everything."

"No, we can't leave."

"You sure?" His tongue teased her lips. He whispered, "You real sure?"

No.

"Daddy, kiss her. Kiss her." Paige beamed. Her hands were filled with cakes and cookies, not to sell, but to eat.

Mikey turned away from her to look at Paige. "You think I should."

"Yes." She looked back at Victoria. "I think she'd like it."

"Paige, we've got to get back to work." She pretended to push him away. "We don't have time for kissing."

Her attention went back to the cookies she nibbled. "Okay." She turned, and vanished back into the front of the trailer.

Mikey stared into her eyes. "So, you don't have time to kiss me?"

"Nope. Too busy." She pushed again, but he didn't move.

"But, what if I do this." He nibbled on her ear. "Or this." His tongue dragged along her jaw from her ear to her mouth.

Surrounded by cakes, cookies, and pies, she had never tasted anything sweeter than the taste of all of them on his lips. His tongue.

Her hands wrapped around his body, holding on—tight. She would never let go again.

Book Club Discussion Guide
Sweet Victory by Angela Kay Austin

• The economy over the last few years has changed the landscape of America. People have had to find ways to supplement their household incomes. Do you know of any creative ways people have managed to keep their bills paid?

• Instead of laying off personnel. A lot of employers have implemented programs like furloughs, and salary cuts. Do you know of any ideas companies have used instead of layoffs?

• Everyone has met someone that they believed was more materialistic than others. Someone trying to "keep up with the Joneses." Victoria James discovers the hard way that her fiancé may not be exactly the most supportive man. Should Victoria have noticed this earlier?

• When Victoria returned home to TN, she was faced with a lot of unfinished business. What other ways could she have dealt with the losses she'd faced?

• A lot of families have to face the choice of live in nurses, assistant living facilities, or moving aging family into their homes. What are the things people should consider when facing this choice?

• Starting your own business is the American dream. What planning should someone interested in running their own business do? What agencies and resources are available to help them?

Free Sweet Victory Companion Cookbook

This Companion Cookbook shares many of the recipes in Sweet Victory, the novel by Angela Kay Austin.

https://www.allromanceebooks.com/product-sweetvictorycompanioncookbook-565997-270.html

More Great Reading
by Angela Kay Austin

Give Me Everything

He'd sat on top of the world... the perfect woman, a daughter, and a job that made his father proud. Now, Kendis was divorced, and his daughter wasn't really his. She'd been through the wringer in her personal life, and now LaKia thinks the only thing she can control is her career. Until Kendis. He gave her everything, and she gave it right back.

On the Frontline
Two Short Stories
Scarlet's Tears and *Derailed*

Angela Kay Austin

Bestselling author Angela Kay Austin has expressed herself through words for as long as she can remember. Poems became songs performed with her cousin at every family gathering. But, eventually, short stories filled her favorite pink diary. An infatuation with music and theater led to years playing various instruments and small extra roles in TV shows before giving way to a degree and career in radio and TV production. After completing another degree in marketing, Angela found herself combining her love for all things creative and worked for many many years in promotions and advertising. But once again, she found herself writing, which led to her first published work which stayed on her publisher's bestseller list for ten weeks. Her second release hit the bestseller list at All Romance eBooks.

She's spoken on author panels, and served on boards for various author groups. When she's not writing, you can find her reading her favorite authors, or researching her next story idea. Angela shares her downtime with her mixed-bred rescue terrier—Midnight, in the beautiful southern state of Tennessee.

She's also a member of Romance Writers of America, From the Heart Romance Writers, Chick Lit Writers of the World, and Washington DC Romance Writers.

www.ingramcontent.com/pod-product-compliance
Lightning Source LLC
Chambersburg PA
CBHW071239130626
46556CB00003B/1080